"I didn't expect to see you so soon."

"Shouldn't you be back at the theatre, trying to put out the fire? Or trying to figure out what happened?"

Rand shrugged. "The blaze is under control. We have to wait for things to cool down before we can start poking around for answers."

Cate gave him a long, measuring look. "You might want to bring the sheriff up to speed tonight rather than tomorrow. He's going to need your help."

Rand leaned forward, his jaw tight, hands itching with a surge of adrenaline. "What kind of help?"

"Professional." She sat up, shoved a hand through the thick mane of hot cocoa-brown waves. "Dad says it wasn't just a fire. It was a meth lab explosion."

Books by Ginny Aiken

Love Inspired Suspense

Mistaken for the Mob
Mixed up with the Mob
Married to the Mob
*Danger in a Small Town
*Suspicion
*Someone to Trust

*Carolina Justice

GINNY AIKEN

is a former newspaper reporter, and lives in Pennsylvania with her engineer husband and their three younger sons—the oldest married and flew the coop. Born in Havana, Cuba, raised in Valencia and Caracas, Venezuela, she discovered books early, and wrote her first novel at age fifteen while she trained with the Ballets de Caracas, later known as the Venezuelan National Ballet. She burned that tome when she turned a "mature" sixteen. Stints as reporter, paralegal, choreographer, language teacher and retail salesperson followed. Her life as wife, mother of four boys and herder of their numerous and assorted friends, brought her back to books and writing in search of her sanity. She's now the author of more than twenty published works and a frequent speaker at Christian women's and writers' workshops, but has yet to catch up with that elusive sanity.

GINNY AIKEN

SOMEONE TO TRUST

Steeple
Hill®

Published by Steeple Hill Books™

STEEPLE HILL BOOKS

Steeple Hill®

Recycling programs for this product may not exist in your area.

ISBN-13: 978-0-373-44346-8

SOMEONE TO TRUST

www.SteepleHill.com

Printed in U.S.A.

In you our fathers put their trust;
they trusted and you delivered them.
—*Psalms* 22:4

ONE

In you our fathers put their trust; They trusted
and you delivered them.

Psalm 22:4 NIV

"Noooo!"

Catelyn Caldwell's cry ripped from her throat as
she slammed her car door. In horror, she watched
flames leap from the old Loganton Theater to the sky.
The stench of devastation seared her nostrils. Fire tinted
the adjacent buildings in shades of angry red as it
writhed and hissed, consuming one of the town's
favorite structures.

The marquee thundered down onto the sidewalk. Its
crash ricocheted off Main Street's buildings, many of
which were the same vintage as the blazing structure.
Firefighters doused the nearest ones to try and keep
them from meeting the same fate as the theater.

Tears burned Cate's eyes, more painful than the
waves of heat slapping her face. Fear shot bile up her
middle. What if…?

"Stop it!" No need to think the worst.

Neal Hunter, one of the oldest and most reliable

firefighters under her dad, had called her not ten minutes earlier. "The theater's on fire and your dad went in after Wilma Tucker." Frustration had made his voice tight. "She wouldn't leave. Said she'd do more good wetting everything down from the inside. Wouldn't listen to reason. Then, when things got bad, I couldn't talk Joe out of going in after her. You might want to head on over here."

As if anything could have kept her away.

Joe Caldwell, Loganton's fire chief, had been putting his life on the line every day since he'd joined the fire department in Roanoke decades earlier. He lived to serve, even if his service kept those who loved him fearing the day when the worst come to pass.

It looked as though today might be that day.

She told herself Dad and Wilma would probably make it out of the raging inferno while she drove there.

Now if she could only make herself believe it.

Tears spilled down Cate's cheeks. She stepped forward, her hands clenched at her sides, her knees buckling. Everything inside her commanded her to run inside, to tear the place apart until she found her father and saw him safe. She didn't want to face the possibility of—

No. She wasn't going there.

Squaring her shoulders, she took a step forward. While she'd been called all kinds of things at different times in her life, she'd never been called a coward.

With every step, her terror at the thought of disaster grew. *I can't, I can't, I can't.*

She'd faced tragedy in the worst way the night her older sister Mandy and her brother-in-law Ross were killed in a car accident eight years ago. She'd had a front-row seat for that nightmare. Cate had been a passenger in the car they'd swerved to avoid.

Surviving that nightmare had taken more than she could stand to surrender again. And yet, because of the nature of her father's work, she might just be forced to give in one more time. And soon.

Her immature faith in Christ had seen her through the aftermath of her sister's death. Her more mature relationship with the Lord these days would see her through again should the worst come to pass.

I can do all things through Christ who strengthens me...

The nearer she got to the burning theater, the more unbearable the heat grew. Cate licked her dry lips and tasted the salt of her tears.

Her dad's men filled the street, water hoses spewing, ladders extended, calling out instructions in tight, intense voices. The silence of the night, an ominous backdrop to all the activity, felt oppressive, threatening.

As she approached the firefighters, Cate's shivers became tides of tremors. When she stepped off the curb a block down and across the street from the blaze, she stumbled and nearly landed on the road.

She took a second to get a grip on her emotions and nerves. At least, she tried—not an easy feat as she scanned the burning building one more time. "Stop thinking the worst," she told herself.

One of the firefighters separated himself from the rest of the team and came toward her. Cate could see the lines of stress on Neal Hunter's face. Under the yellow hard hat, her dad's best friend's face glistened with sweat. She called out his name.

He trotted the last few steps toward her. "I'm hoping the guys will turn the corner with this monster soon. I don't think it's spreading anymore."

At the thought of what she had to ask, she shook harder. "Has he…have you seen him?"

The flash of pain across Neal's face said everything she needed to know.

"Do you think there's any chance Dad's still…?"

His eyes blazed as bright as the flames. "There's every chance, Cate. The fire is worse in one spot in the basement. I figure Joe yanked Wilma away from dumping buckets on it and dragged her to the safer area at the back. Don't ever give up hope."

The smile she tried to give him wobbled around the edges as his words registered. "So the blaze started down there, away from the patrons."

"Looks that way. Don't think we're looking at kids smoking in the john or anything like that."

"Does the theater have a problem with teen smokers?"

"Not really, but the high school seniors came to watch a film for English tonight. All one hundred twenty-nine of them were here. Them, and their chaperones."

"But the fire didn't start in the bathroom."

Neal shook his head. "Gotta get back, Cate. I'll let you know as soon as I know anything."

Another firefighter ran up. "If we don't turn this around in the next five minutes, I'm going to call in the other counties' departments."

Neal glanced at the theater. "Maybe you shouldn't wait."

The flames bathed the newcomer's face with an angry glow, but Cate still recognized him. In spite of the stress, soot and sweat, she had to acknowledge that the years since he'd left town had been good to Randall Mason. Then again, he'd always been drop-dead gorgeous, popular, athletic…

Everything Cate hadn't been.

Rand had also been the person she most loved to hate in school.

"Any sign of Wilma or the chief?" he asked.

Cate dragged in a harsh breath.

Neal glared and jerked his head in the universal sign for let's talk about this over *there.* "Not on our side—yet."

But the captain didn't seem to hear Neal—he was staring at Cate. Her instinctive response to his question had caught his attention. His blue eyes homed in on her. "I thought you guys had cleared the perimeter. We can't have civilians this near to an active fire."

Cate tipped up her chin. "I'm not your usual civilian. Neal called to tell me Dad had gone in after Wilma. We're hoping they made it to the back of the basement, since Neal says the damage is not supposed to be as bad there."

"Cate? Catey Caldwell…is that you?"

Her mouth curved up on one side. "The one and only."

"You've changed—" He winced as he realized how his words sounded. "I'm sorry."

"It's okay. I have changed. Believe me, I know. Let's face it. I think the last time you saw me I had green hair. Or maybe that week it was purple."

"Something like that."

She offered him a tentative smile, hard though it was to eke out. "You don't have to dance around reality with me. I'm more aware than anyone else of the dangers you guys face. And even though it took hours of arguing, I finally got Dad to agree to have one of his men call me if…well, if there was ever any possibility of…" She waved toward the remains of the theater. "Neal did me the favor."

Rand's expression warmed with compassion. "If there's one thing I know, it's that your father's one of the smartest, best-trained and most capable men I know. If there's even the smallest corner left standing in the back of that place, then I'm sure he's found his way there. Took Wilma with him, too. Have faith."

The last two words rang in her heart. Faith…these days she had plenty of that. A glance at the theater encouraged her. It looked as though her father's men had managed to contain the worst of the flames to the lobby. Until the blaze had erupted, that lobby had sparkled with the chrome and crystal Wilma had lavished on the place during the recent renovation.

Cate closed her eyes and offered a silent prayer.

"Hey!" someone called over the crackle of fire and rush of water. "We found them! They're alive! Get the ambulances over here!"

Tears again poured down Cate's face. "Thank you, Jesus."

Rand looked at Cate, the surprise in his blue eyes mirroring what she had grown used to seeing over the years. Those who'd known her as a rebellious teen had trouble recognizing her as the responsible woman she'd become.

She forced another tight smile. "Surprise, surprise."

As she hurried off in the direction of her father, she heard him say, "And how."

Rand loped back to help the men pull out Joe and Wilma, both of whom were suffering with smoke inhalation, numerous burns and unknown internal injuries from the collapse of a portion of the theater's ceiling.

He'd feared for his mentor's life, in spite of the men's training and their determination to save the popular chief, as they'd carefully removed chunks of ceiling off the two trapped victims. When they were finally freed, Rand realized his hands were shaking. It was far more gut-wrenching to fight to save people he'd known his whole life than strangers back in Charlotte. He'd wanted a more personal touch, and so he'd come home. He hadn't expected this level of closeness.

Thankfully, Joe and Wilma were out. "Hang in there," he told the older man as the EMTs strapped him to the gurney. "They'll get you back to fighting form in no time at the hospital."

Joe tried to grin, but instead grimaced as the gurney rolled away. Rand glanced at Cate. Sympathy swelled when he noticed her expression. It hovered somewhere between despair and hope.

He heard her sob, watched her bring a fist to her mouth. Her misery drew him.

As he approached, his steps slow and tired, he ran a hand down his sweat-dampened face. A glance at his hand showed traces of soot—a common job hazard. He swiped it against his tan gear, then realized the action might have made matters worse.

The closer Rand went, the more intently he watched her. With her tangled hair, long-sleeved Tarheel Basketball T-shirt, drawstring flannel pants and running shoes with a hole in the right toe, she looked appealing in a true girl-next-door way. She'd obviously changed into sleepwear before she'd received Neal's call and had rushed out to her father's side. It seemed Cate loved her father as much as Rand knew Joe loved her.

"Hey," he said. "I just spoke to one of the EMTs. They don't mind if you ride with Joe in the ambulance. I figured you'd want to."

The breath she drew sounded ragged, rough and heavy, maybe with the dissipating smoke. "To be honest, I didn't get so far as to think about that. I'm kind of numb. All I could think about was that Dad had survived. Thanks for getting him out."

"No problem—and I didn't do it single-handed." He glanced toward the ambulance. "I'd like to go see how he's doing, but I have to stay here and step into his shoes—an impossible challenge—but he hired me to be his number two, and I owe him my best on the job. That, and to make sure he gets to the hospital as soon as possible. With you at his side."

A strange undercurrent flew between them. Cate stood taller. "I'm sure you'll get a chance to visit him soon enough."

He shrugged. "Yeah. I'll be there as soon as I can."

"Well, thanks. Again." As she started toward the ambulance, she gave him a last look over her shoulder, a slight smile on her lips. "I'm sure I'll see you around the hospital."

She hurried off to the ambulance, and Rand stood

still for a second or two. What had she seen when she'd turned to look at him? It had made her smile…sort of. For a moment, he wished he still looked like the popular football team captain and Honor Society member he'd once been, the guy she probably remembered from high school.

On the other hand, maybe when she looked at him, Cate saw the arson investigator for the Charlotte Fire Department he'd been in the years between high school and his recent return. He wondered if she'd heard all the stories that seemed to have mushroomed in town. Winnie Zook, the town's most avid gossip, had been heard telling those who'd listen that Rand had come back to the slower-paced Loganton Fire Department not just to put out fires, but to follow in his father's footsteps and sell books on his own time. As soon as he'd started knocking around in his father's old bookstore, tearing down walls and sawing at all hours—when not on duty, of course—Winnie had taken to stopping by to chat. She'd also made a point of strolling past the plate glass window and peeking in every so often, since the former Reading Corner sat next to her knitting goods store.

Rand had no idea what he was going to do with his father's old store, but remodeling the space gave him something to do in his downtime. He sure wasn't going to bother arguing with Winnie, much less those others who insisted he'd come home to write the Great American Novel, based on his experiences. Or even with those Logantonians who just knew he was hiding out from the mob—he had helped put away a number of organized crime types who torched property for the insurance pay-off, after all.

The multiple theories, creative as they were, made Rand laugh. He'd come back home because it was home. He knew everyone in town, and he wanted to make a difference in their lives. True, he'd left all those years ago for practically the same reason. A family tragedy had turned his life upside down. His cousin Ross's death had been hard to take, especially since it had been Rand's first call as a rookie volunteer fire-fighter. He hadn't wanted to face the loss of another person he loved, or even knew.

In time, he'd realized he was lonely in Charlotte. So he'd come back. Now, he'd faced the very issue that had sent him running in the first place. And he'd dealt with it. He hoped it grew easier as he went along. He'd have to ask Joe for advice once the older man was well enough.

But he sure couldn't tell the citizens he'd been hired to protect why he'd left as a young man. Or why he'd come back. It might make him sound pathetic, certainly not strong enough to keep them safe.

The ambulance door slammed shut behind Cate. He wondered which of the lurid tales about him she'd heard, what she'd thought of him. Had she seen a competent firefighter, her father's second in command, a successful professional concerned about a man who'd been there for him when Rand had needed comfort and guidance after his father died?

He and Cate had never had much in common. She'd been a flake; he'd been serious, studious, driven. But tonight, those differences didn't matter.

Rand glanced back at the burnt building. The moon-light highlighted the shell that remained of the vintage structure against the smoky sky. What a loss. Buildings like the theater were vanishing treasures. He hated seeing them like this.

At least no lives had been lost. Joe and Wilma should, with good medical care, recover.

As he headed back toward his clustered men, the image of Cate's face flashed through his thoughts. He felt the sudden urge to hurry to the hospital, to tell her Joe would be fine, to comfort her in her time of need.

He had no earthly idea why the urge was so strong. He just knew he wanted to see Cate again.

The ambulance pulled away from the scene, siren blaring, the EMTs working on her father. Cate shrank into herself, tried to take up the least amount of the limited space. As random medical equipment bleeped and flashed, she watched her dad's face.

He'd open his eyes for a moment, then, obviously drained, he'd surrender and his eyelids would droop back down. The next time he opened them again, she saw him look around, work to focus and when he spotted her, struggle to raise his head.

Ann Davies, one of the EMTs, turned to Cate. "He's trying to say something, but the mask is in the way. He needs the oxygen right now, though."

Her father's urge to communicate encouraged Cate. "Can you lift the mask for a second? Just enough for him to talk."

Tethered to the narrow gurney, Joe Caldwell, a huge bear of a man, dwarfed the tight confines of the ambulance. As Ann considered Cate's request, he grew more agitated.

Cate tried again. "He's upset. Let him tell us what he wants and then he'll probably settle back down. He's a pretty stubborn guy."

With a final measuring glance at Joe, Ann gave Cate a nod. "Come closer, right down here so he can whisper."

Cate couldn't have imagined what her father finally said.

"Not just fire…" he said in a wheezy, scratchy whisper. "Explosion…meth lab in the front of the basement…"

"Meth lab!" In the last year and a half, Loganton had seen the drug make inroads into the community. True, a meth lab had been found and a couple of dealers jailed, but not before the drug had claimed its victims.

Hopefully, it wouldn't claim an additional two tonight.

Dad was a fighter and Wilma Tucker a spunky livewire with more stubborn to her than a mule. By God's merciful grace they'd both recover.

Cate brought her lips close to his ear as Ann replaced the mask on her father's face. "I'll call the PD and the sheriff's office as soon as we get to the hospital. I'm sure they're planning to talk to you, but this'll make them get right to it. All you have to do is relax and recover."

His eyes blazed. He twisted against the gurney's restraints. Ann lifted the mask again.

"No time to lay around—the kids! You're the boss now, Catey. But the fire…"

The EMT clapped the mask back in place, chuckled and shook her head. "Sorry, Chief. You don't get a choice here. Cate'll do her thing with your grandkids, but you're gonna have to let your men do the footwork this time. And that mask doesn't move again, you hear?"

Sympathy flooded Cate. There was nothing that got her dad more energized than digging out clues to a fire's cause. This time, he'd have to trust others to do the job. Like Rand, the former Charlotte arson investigator he'd hired as his number two man.

Her dad's job now was to stay quiet and recover. Although he wasn't out of the woods yet, relief flooded Cate. This, she could handle.

Another thought flew into her head. The kids. Total responsibility for ten-year-olds Robby and Tommy, and eight-year-old Lindsay. Could she handle *that?*

Only time would tell.

At the hospital, Rand headed for the ER entrance. He had to see how Wilma was doing. He'd worked part-time at the theater for her parents as a teen—collecting tickets, sweeping floors, serving popcorn—and he'd come to care deeply for them. Wilma herself? Well, she'd been interesting, that's for sure.

A free spirit all her life, Wilma left Loganton after graduation and wandered back home whenever an adventure came to its end, only to leave again once the lure of the open road—and a new adventure—became too potent to ignore. She'd finally come to stay when her mother's rheumatoid arthritis grew too painful for her to keep working and her father lost his battle with macular degeneration and went blind.

The older Tuckers had moved into the Pines Retirement Community on the outskirts of Loganton, and Wilma had restored the theater to its lush, roaring-twenties original glory. Rand knew Augie and Ruth Tucker would have a hard time coping with their daughter's injuries and the devastation of their family business.

At the information desk, he asked about Wilma and was told to take a seat in the waiting room. Doctors were working on her and a nurse would give him an update once the desk was notified of her condition.

As he dropped into the maroon armchair, his thoughts flew back to the conversation he'd had with Neal while the EMTs loaded Joe and Wilma into the ambulances.

Rand couldn't figure out what might have started the fire—yet. Neal had said it looked as though the blaze had begun in the basement, toward the front of the building. Wilma must have taken longer than usual closing up after the seven-forty-five showing.

From his days working for the Tuckers, Rand knew the basement was practically empty. A cinder-block wall with a metal door in the middle blocked off the area under the lobby. Augie Tucker had developed black and white photos there years ago, but he'd sold the equipment and emptied out the space when his eyes had started to fail sometime during Rand's junior year in college. He couldn't see how the fire had started where Neal suspected—nothing flammable had been kept there.

Of course, Wilma could have started storing things in the basement after taking over the theater. Nothing fed a fire better than piles of junk. But the thought of Wilma—the original minimalist who'd lived most of her adult years out of a backpack—storing junk was almost laughable.

Rand's gut told him there was more to that fire

than just fire. While common sense reminded him of the building's age and dry condition, years of fighting and investigating fires had left him with a good nose for trouble.

He looked up at the sound of footsteps. Cate walked into the waiting room. Before he could stop himself, he asked. "Where are the kids?"

"The kids? You mean the twins and Lindsay?"

"Of course. I hope you didn't just run out on them."

Her brows drew close and her lips tightened. "I'd never leave three little kids alone. No matter how scared I was about Dad. Miss Tabitha's with them."

"They'll be scared about their grandfather, don't you think?"

"Once I hear how he's doing, I'll go home and make sure they know he's going to…going to be okay."

The wobble in Cate's voice told him how scared *she* was. Sympathy again filled him, but before he could say anything, she went on.

"You didn't really expect me to stay tucked under my blanket while Dad's life was on the line, did you?"

The shine of tears brightened her chocolate eyes. Maybe he'd been too hard on her. He knew she loved her father. And Joe had told Rand a number of times how much Cate had changed, how responsible she was.

She probably also loved her niece and nephews and Rand was glad to know she'd arranged for Miss Tabitha, one of Loganton's true pillars, to stay with the youngsters. But as wonderful as Miss Tabitha was, she was quite an elderly woman. Was she up to watching two ten-year-old boys? An eight-year-old girl?

Now that Joe Caldwell was injured, Rand would

have to make sure the kids didn't lack supervision. He owed as much to their late father, his older cousin Ross. In the interest of keeping peace, he decided not to say anything more to Cate about the kids. He'd just do what he thought best for them.

Rand hadn't had much contact with them while he worked in Charlotte, but with Joe as their guardian, he knew they'd been in good hands. But now? Rand wasn't about to just leave them in Cate's care without at least checking up on their well-being.

"I didn't expect to see you again so soon," she said in the growing silence.

Rand shrugged. "The blaze is under control and the guys can finish up. I'm sure you know we have to wait for things to cool down before we can start looking for answers." He shot a glance toward the large double doors to the ER. "The Tuckers are like family to me. I want to know how Wilma's doing before I go out to the Pines to tell her folks."

She arched a brow. "You're going to tell them? I would have thought the new police chief would do that."

"I told Neal to let the PD know I wanted to be the one to talk to them. I don't want to see any more of the Tuckers in the hospital. It's going to hit them hard, and if Chief Rodgers just shows up, it could make things worse."

In a gesture full of exhaustion, Cate tipped her head back against her chair, her eyes closed but her features tense. "You might still want to take Ethan Rodgers with you when you go talk to them. After what happened tonight, I suspect they're going to see a lot of him in his official capacity during the next few weeks."

His gut tightened and he knew his initial instinct had been right on target. "What's going on?"

Through half-closed eyelids, she gave him a long, measuring look. "Ethan's going to need your help."

Rand leaned forward, hands itching with the surge of adrenaline he always felt when a hunch paid off. "What kind of help?"

"Professional." She sat up, shoved a hand through the thick mane of hot cocoa-brown waves. "Dad says it wasn't just a fire. He says a meth lab blew up."

Nose for trouble? His was dead on.

From the moment he'd arrived at the theater, his instincts had begun to alert him and not just to the scent of crime. They had tipped him off to something he hadn't expected. He'd come home looking for a more peaceful, less stressful work environment. As an arson investigator, he'd had his fill of arsonists, a unique kind of thief and killer who took pleasure from the destruction they caused. And now, after the first serious fire he worked for the Loganton Fire Department, it turned out the thrill of the hunt still gave him a charge.

He stood. "Meth's a killer—in more ways than one. Any idea who might be behind it?"

She shook her head and arched her brow. "Here I thought the answer to that question was what an arson investigation was all about."

He conceded her point with a nod. Then he spun and headed out to find his answer. His mind whirled with the new information. What Cate had just told him colored the fire at the theater in a whole different palette.

There was a killer out there. He hadn't killed Joe or

Wilma, but anyone who cooked meth had blood on his hands, the blood of those he had hooked.

Rand realized he would have missed solving arson cases had there really been a difference between a small town and a large city. But people were people. A kaleidoscope of memories swirled through his head. Loss, injury, death—and the cesspool where arsonists lived and where he'd had to swim all those years to catch them. And yet, here he was, treading that same water again.

The constant contact with the worst side of society had nearly stolen every last drop of humanity he'd possessed. That's why he'd come home…

…never thinking he'd wind up right back in the thick of it.

TWO

At six the next morning, Zoe Donovan, Cate's best friend since kindergarten, finished her shift at the hospital blood lab. She marched right up to the ICU and insisted Cate leave with her. Cate tried to argue.

Zoe countered. "I'm not listening. The kids will be up any minute now and you know they're going to squabble. Think of poor Miss Tabitha, all alone with the three darlings."

Cate glared. "They do go at it with all the gusto of sibling rivalry, but Miss Tabitha is wonderful with them and I just checked in with her forty-five minutes ago. She said she had everything under control and I shouldn't worry. She's such a sweetheart. They're always on their best behavior for her. This is Dad—"

"And he would want you home. His medical team's fabulous—you know he's in excellent hands. Tell me I'm wrong. Go on." The light of challenge shone in her green eyes. "Besides, just think of all the times you and your dad have had to referee the trio just to wind up with something that might remind you of peace."

"Fine. I'm a realist. They're wonderful individuals, but perfect? Uh-uh. Especially not during the morning routine."

Cate tugged her jacket tighter around her middle when they stepped out into the cold fall morning. "So how am I going to tell them their gramps is in critical condition? They've already gone through so much. First they lost their parents, then their grandmother three years later. Now this."

"The Lord will find a way—or in this case, a word. Ask Him. He won't let you down."

"But this is *Dad.*" She closed her eyes, shook her head, took a breath. "The kids are little and he's the only stability they've ever known."

"That's probably why he asked you to move back in a couple of years ago."

Cate snorted. "You know he doesn't need my help. And all that babble about my youth helping him parent them better than he would alone is just that: babble."

Everyone in town had commented on his apparent lunacy. Predictions had hovered somewhere between the kids' certain ruination and their imminent stints in the juvie system.

Their perceptions of Cate hadn't changed much over the years. Even if she had. Or she thought she had.

"What if…what if all the people who said I couldn't cut it were right? What if I blow it with them and something awful happens?"

"Come on. Look at your day care center."

"That's different. Parents know I hire only the best. They know their kids are safe with my teachers, some of whom they've known for years. I'm mainly the administrator. But Lindsay and the twins? Dad's always been there to keep me from messing up too badly."

Zoe brushed imaginary lint off Cate's shoulder. "Dust that junk off, sister. I remember how scared you were, but it didn't take you long to get into a family groove and you've done a great job, if I do say so myself."

They crossed the parking lot, heading for Zoe's yellow subcompact. Cate loved the tiny car, especially since she had to tool around town in a massive green minivan.

Zoe pulled out her keys and zapped the lock gizmo. "Hop in. I'll give you a ride back to your car."

They pulled out into the light early morning traffic in silence. A moment later, Zoe piped up. Again.

"What'd you think of your dad's newest hire?"

Rand's features flew into Cate's thoughts, vivid and strong. He'd changed, but not so much. He still reminded her of her dad's protégé, the guy who could never do wrong back in high school.

Only better looking.

But she couldn't let Zoe know she thought of Rand that way. "Eh…not much. He's still Rand Mason, you know?"

"He did come to see about your dad. He cares."

Cate shrugged. "He's always cared about Dad. Of course he'd come see how Dad's doing."

At the light, Zoe shot her a sideways glance. "Hm…just to see about your dad? Didn't look like it to me."

Intense blue eyes materialized in Cate's memory. "Um…yeah. He gave me the third degree about the kids. He doesn't think much of me."

Zoe gunned the pedal. "Coulda fooled me. He

looked pretty interested when he was talking to you right before I got there."

"No way! Not Rand. He's not interested in me. He doesn't like me. Trust me. A woman can tell when a man can't stand her. He can't stand me."

"Uh-huh." Zoe chuckled, and Cate's frustration grew. Rand had made her uncomfortable. But arguing with Zoe was a no-win situation. Besides, she had three kids waiting for her. And Cate knew all about the weight of parental responsibility. The fire had made hers even greater.

Cate glared at her friend. "Just drive, will ya? I've had a horrible night, my dad's in the ICU, and the three kids are probably driving Miss Tabitha nuts by now. That's the only thing I can do anything about right now, so let me get going to do what I can."

"The lady doth protest—"

"Do you think Dad's really going to be okay? I'm afraid…" She drew a deep breath. "I have to trust the hospital with Dad's life. That's just all there is to it. And they'd better not let me down. I'm not ready to do this parenting thing all on my own all of the time."

"Get over yourself, girl. You're gonna do it, you're gonna do it fine and you're not gonna do it alone, not while he's in the hospital and not when he comes home. You have friends who'll help, like me. I'm not chopped liver, you know. Besides, the Lord's gonna be right there with you, remember?"

"Yeah. I remember. I just want Dad home again."

Zoe slowed to pull up behind the van. When she shifted the car into idle, she reached out and put a gentle hand on Cate's arm. "And your dad *will* be home again. Have faith. And a little bit of trust won't hurt either."

Tears welled in Cate's eyes. "You're right. Faith and trust, faith and trust. Got it."

They said their goodbyes and she headed for the van, her gaze on the rosy tint of the eastern sky. As the day became more real, details crossed her mind. Had Robby run the dishwasher last night? He often forgot to follow through on his chores. She decided it would have to be a cereal morning. Tommy would likely howl, because he loved his pancakes, but no way was she about to cook anything when she got home.

Lindsay would take the news about her grandfather harder than the twins. She was the youngest, only an infant when her parents had died, but that wasn't really the issue. Sweet Lindsay had a quiet nature, so much so as to seem almost withdrawn much of the time. She teared up at sappy commercials and she was shier than one of Miss Tabitha's night-blooming primroses.

As much as she loved her niece, Cate struggled to understand someone so different from her. She'd always prided herself on her tough and scrappy approach to life.

Another pang of uncertainty pierced her. Was she really up to raising three kids? Her schedule usually kept her too busy to think about such things, so she did what she had to do to keep life moving along its regular tracks. Now, with Dad's serious injuries, she'd been derailed. She was going to be on her own. Would she fail and prove all the town gossips right?

Ten feet away from the van, she caught a glimpse of herself in a shop window. The dark shadows under her eyes made her look as though she needed a doctor herself. Her cheeks lacked color and her hair resembled tangled ropes of taffy—the real thing, not the carnival-style, rainbow colored kind. Even though once upon a time, rainbow hair *had* been her thing, as Rand had reminded her. She sighed.

Still, rainbow hair or not, she didn't look like she could be trusted to babysit, much less raise Mandy's kids. Why Dad had thought she should, why he'd decided to trust her with his beloved grandchildren, she'd never know. Not that he had much choice now, thanks to his injuries.

Fear struck. Her knees wobbled and she leaned against the side of the van, her mind going a mile a minute.

Dad had always been calm and competent when the kids' needs threatened to overwhelm Cate. But now that she thought about it, he'd started to turn the day-to-day stuff over to her almost the moment she moved back in. He'd said more than once that the kids would grow her up now that she'd become their stand-in mom. So far, she didn't really feel all that different, but she had learned one very valuable truth: motherhood was not for wimps.

When she opened her eyes, the blackened theater loomed before her. The events of the night tugged at her and she didn't resist. She made her way to the old structure, then just stood and stared, letting the sadness and anger wash over her.

Who? Who'd been making poison to feed to the town's youth? Who would destroy this beautiful building? Who would have risked people's lives? And for nothing more than pure greed.

Cate thought of Loganton's residents. She'd grown up in town, so she knew everyone. Even guided by suspicion, she couldn't come up with one potential guilty soul.

But someone was guilty. Dad and Wilma were in the ICU.

As far as she was concerned, whoever was behind the meth lab was going down. Cate would do everything in her power to see to it. Even if she had to find the culprit herself.

As awkward as she felt around him, she was glad Rand had come back to town. His arson investigation experience should serve the fire department well. But if he came up with no answers, well, then she'd just dig up those answers herself.

Well aware that she shouldn't, Cate slipped under the yellow tape and walked up to the theater. The tall glass doors wore a thick coat of black soot on the inside and she couldn't look through them as she'd loved to do ever since her parents had taken her and Mandy to a special Mother's Day showing of *The Sound of Music*. She'd always loved the theater, and movies of all kinds.

Cupping her hands, Cate blocked the growing sunlight and leaned closer to the door. The soot layer did make it impossible to see, even from this vantage point. As she strained, she heard a sound to her right. She didn't see anything unusual, but still couldn't stop herself from pursuing her curiosity. She rounded the corner and arrived at the main exit. A montage of memories flew through her head. She remembered all the films she'd watched inside with her girlfriends.

After the show, they'd leave in a cluster, giggling if they'd watched a comedy, sniffling if it had been a heart-tugger of some kind.

All so innocent, in stark contrast to what the basement had most recently housed.

The steel door was locked. No evidence of the fire on this side of the building. Even the sidewalk was clear. Clear but for a piece of trash three feet past the side door.

Cate went to pick it up, but when she leaned down, she froze. The trash turned out to be a twisted lump of plastic, blackened by the fire. From the top, a metal clip, the kind on cheap key chains, stuck straight out as though pointing to the theater.

A quick glance up and down the sidewalk revealed no other debris, nothing. And while she didn't give it much importance, Cate couldn't discount what she'd found, either. One of the firefighters might have dropped it when he'd carried something else from inside the building, and it might be relevant to the investigation.

She couldn't ignore it. Nor could she pick it up. As the daughter of a firefighter, she knew better. So she reached for her phone to dial the station.

Next thing she knew, a blow to the back of her head knocked her off her feet. She smashed her forehead against the sidewalk.

"Oh!" Her eyes filled with sudden tears. Behind her, footsteps pelted away. She scrambled upright, then stumbled in the direction they'd gone. "Hey! What was that about?"

By the time she reached the corner, there was no one

in sight. Cate rubbed her forehead, and then wiped the tears from her eyes.

A cold shiver ran through her. Had she interrupted something? Had she seen something she shouldn't have?

Maybe someone had not wanted to be seen near the theater. Had her presence threatened the meth dealer? Or had he just wanted to make sure she didn't see him at the scene of his crimes?

It didn't matter. Not right then. What mattered was to get someone with experience to take a look at that…that plastic thing. Cate followed through with her earlier start, and dialed the P.D. They asked her a handful of questions, then promised to send help.

Cate drew a bracing breath in preparation for what she had to do next. She dialed the fire station.

Rand answered, exhaustion in his voice. When she identified herself, he asked if she planned on sleeping.

"Not yet, but soon. Zoe Donovan gave me a ride to the van when she finished her shift. I…uhm…stopped to look at the theater, and found something strange near the side exit. Thought you might want to see it before people start walking around later this morning. Do you think it might be important?"

In a tight voice, ripe with disapproval, he asked her to describe her discovery. When she finished, he didn't answer right away.

"Can't tell you much about it right now," he finally said. "But no matter whether it's important or not, it's something for us to look at, not you. Last I remember, there was yellow tape around the theater. As the fire chief's daughter, you know that means stay away. Don't touch the plastic thing, and stay put till I get there. I'm on my way."

Great. Yet another chance to come face-to-face with Rand's disapproval.

But she'd deal with Rand's attitude some other time. Right then, the only thing that mattered was finding the creep who'd built the meth lab in the basement of the Loganton Theater.

The one who'd almost killed Wilma and her dad.

Rand tried to contain his irritation as he stared at Cate. "And you just decided to duck under the tape and walk around an arson fire investigation for…what? The fun of it?"

She didn't like his comment. Fire blazed from her dark eyes. "Not for the fun of it. That's ridiculous."

"Then tell me again why you were on the premises."

"I wasn't on the premises. Not exactly." She blew a wavy strand of tawny hair from her forehead. "I came to get the van, and walked up to the theater. It's so sad how, after all these years, it's ruined now. I started to remember all the shows I watched here."

The way she clamped down her lips told him how much he'd irritated her, but that was too bad. He wasn't sure he believed her story. He didn't know if she'd told him everything she knew. "Ahem!"

His less-than-subtle nudge got her going again. "Then I walked down the side street. That's when I saw the…that blob. Even I could tell it had been burnt, so I went to see what it might be. I didn't touch it, but while I was looking, someone came up from behind, and knocked me to the ground. Do you think they were trying to scare me away?"

"Someone? Knocked you to the ground?" What was she trying to pull? An early morning attacker?

She rubbed the middle of her forehead, and now that he looked, he could see a red bump, maybe a scrape, right where she'd placed her fingers. He waited for her answer.

She shrugged. "Someone knocked me over. I don't know why. I just know I didn't touch the plastic, and I didn't trip myself. No one else came by."

Her expression, her tone of voice, her body language were all consistent, still… "Coincidences don't happen in my line of work."

Her eyes narrowed, and she clamped her lips tight. She wasn't happy with his response, certainly not his skepticism. Too bad. It was part of who he was, the job he had to do. And part of dealing with her—the past, memories and all that baggage.

"The only thing I can do," she said, her voice earnest and serious, "is tell you the truth. It's up to you whether you believe me or not. I hope you do."

As Cate stood before him, a flash of remembrance took him back eight years. He'd spotted her across the street from his cousin's mangled vehicle, Lindsay in her arms, the twin boys on either side. But moments before he got to the scene, moments before the children's mother and father had died, she'd been in the car that caused the wreck. A car driven by the boy-friend who'd had too much to drink.

Rand couldn't say if there was any chance he'd ever believe her. So it was best to get on with the task before him. He jiggled a plastic baggie containing the melted lump. "This thing's going out for testing. I'm sure once the lab gets a handle on what it might be, I'll have more questions for you. I'll see you then."

He took off, then remembered the scrape on her forehead. He stopped, turned to face her again. "Are you okay? Do you need me to call the ambulance? That looks…sore."

She glared and shook her head. "I don't need your help. I can take care of myself. Just find out who did this."

He nodded, spun and walked away, the touch of her angry stare as though it were a flame against his back.

Ten minutes after Rand Mason walked away outside the theater, Cate again tamped down her anger and guided the van up the long drive at the old Caldwell place. The white house with black shutters had once been the heart of a real farm. Cate's great-grandparents had sold a hefty chunk of the land during the Great Depression, and then, over the years, her grandparents and finally Mom and Dad had sold off the rest of the fields. No one had been interested in raising chickens or growing crops.

The families who'd bought the land hadn't purchased it for farming, either. Many had built minimansions, which by contrast made the Caldwell place and the handful of other vintage homes left on the road seem older than they really were. But the Caldwell place never looked shabby or neglected. Dad wouldn't have let it, even if he'd had to slave over the property every minute he spent away from the station to get the work done.

Cate dragged herself up the porch steps and unlocked the door. The scent of home surrounded her. Furniture polish, fabric softener and a lingering hint of the cinnamon rolls she'd baked the day before mingled into a perfume that brought tears to her eyes with its familiarity.

Miss Tabitha Cranston, the sweet older woman who ran a boarding house in town and to whom she'd turned for help when Neal had called, hurried to hug her. "How is he?"

"Not good, but fighting."

"That's the Joe we all know and love." She slipped her arms into her ivory colored cardigan, picked up her handbag and stepped onto the porch. "Oh, dear! Will you look at your forehead? What happened?"

Almost as if with a will of its own, her hand flew up to touch the sore spot. The whole episode still made her uneasy, but she didn't think it would be a good idea to worry Miss Tabitha any further.

"Oh, it's nothing much. Don't worry. I just didn't watch where I was walking this morning, and I tripped on the sidewalk. I'll be okay."

Miss Tabitha tsk-tsked. "Make sure you put ice on it, okay?"

When Cate nodded, the older woman murmured more comforting words, then headed down the steps. "I'll be praying. We all will."

Robby's early morning grumble startled Cate. "Where you been?"

"Where are the others?"

The ten-year-old gave her a one-sided shrug. "Dunno."

The Caldwells weren't known for their morning verve. "Have you seen them? Are they up yet?"

Lindsay wafted down the stairs. "Tommy's in the bathroom. I can't get him out and I need my shower."

"Use mine." Cate made a mental note to deal with the bathroom situation later. At the foot of the stairs, she leaned on the newel post and gave the missing twin a bellow. "Get down here, Thomas Caldwell Mason. You can't monopolize the bathroom."

From the depths of the hall bathroom came a wail with a growl. She took it to mean her nephew had heard her, didn't care for her comment, but was on his way…on his terms. Good. She didn't feel she could recount last night's events more than once.

Shoulders squared, she headed for the kitchen.

Moments later, the bathroom monopolizer shuffled to the table. "You make eggs?"

"Not today, kiddo." She opened the refrigerator. "It's a cereal day."

He groaned.

"You guys are going to have to work with me here." She turned and plunked the gallon of milk in the middle of the table. "I have to talk to you."

Robby's dark eyes grew wide. "Mrs. Washburn called you? She promised she wouldn't if I did two extra weeks of cleanup duty…"

At Cate's frown, his words dried up. It was a good thing the kid had no internal editor—he gave himself away all the time. "Cleanup duty?"

He winced, clamped his mouth shut, then shrugged.

Swell. "What'd you do this time, Robert? That poor woman. The least you can do is go easy on her."

The scowl was classic little-boy-in-trouble. "I didn't do nothing."

Cate sighed. She'd have to call the teacher. Again.

At the head of the table, she laced her fingers and offered a brief, silent prayer for strength and the right words. Then, out loud, she asked the Lord to bless their food. After the Amens, she turned back to Robby. "We'll deal with Mrs. Washburn later, okay?"

His relief would have made her smile if she weren't so worried about the kids' reactions to the news about Dad.

"I told you guys I had to talk to you."

Six eyes zeroed in on her face. Robby frowned. Tommy crossed his arms. Lindsay shrank.

"Gramps had to work a fire last night. Mr. Hunter called me when things got dangerous. Turns out the theater on Main Street burned down and Gramps was trying to get Miss Tucker out of danger. They got hurt—pretty badly—when debris fell on them."

One lone tear ran down Lindsay's cheek.

"Why's he gotta do such a crazy job?" Tommy griped.

Robby stuck out his chin as far as it would go. "He's not dead, is he?"

Lindsay gasped, shoved her chair away from the table, and ran out of the room. Cate stood to follow.

The twins chose to bicker.

"Way to go, pigeon-brain."

"Didn't do nothing, monkey-breath."

Time to be the grown-up. "Of course Gramps isn't dead," Cate said. "He's at the hospital and they've stuck a bunch of tubes into him, but he's going to make it. He's just going to have a long recovery ahead of him."

Robby melted back in his chair. "That works."

Not so much for Tommy. "How soon's he coming home?"

"I don't know, kiddo. But that converted garage workshop of his is going to be off limits while he's on the mend. And I'm going to need your help around the house while I fix up the living room so he doesn't have to worry about stairs to get to his bedroom."

"I'm not cleaning no toilets." Robby hated bathroom duty.

"'Any' Robby. 'Any toilets,'" she corrected. "We'll work around the toilets." She pretended to consider. "I know! You can take over trash can washup detail. You'll remember to get all the crud out, won't you? Use lots of bleach, right?"

His eyes bulged and he shook his head.

She grinned. "Later, okay? Now I have to go check on your sister and grab a shower. Eat up or you'll both be late for school."

Tommy's eyes twinkled with mischief. "But we can't go to school today, Aunt Cate. Not with Gramps in the hospital. We gotta go see him, cheer him up, you know?"

"Nice try, bud. No go, though. Gramps is going to be in the hospital for a long time and you aren't going to miss any school over it. I'll take you to see him once you get out this afternoon."

"But Aunt Catey—"

"No buts, babe. Time to rock 'n' roll."

The boys moved. Slowly, but they moved. Things hadn't gone as badly as they might have. Cate had known Lindsay would take it hard and she'd been prepared to talk to the girl, pray with her and help her deal with her fears. The boys…well, they were a handful, but they'd taken the news fairly well.

That's when it hit her. How was she going to be in two places at one time? She'd never left the kids unsupervised until last night and then only for a handful of minutes and because Dad's life was on the line. She'd left only when she knew Miss Tabitha was in the car and on her way over.

That was why Rand's suggestion that she might not be able to handle the kids rankled so much. Why had he echoed the town gossips? She'd had to put up with all that ever since she came home. She hadn't needed him to repeat it.

If she was perfectly honest, it had stung much more coming from Rand than from the gossips. She couldn't deny it; there was a heightened tension between them, a push and pull, a certain intensity she'd never experienced before.

From the deepest corners of her mind, a thought niggled. Had Zoe been right? Was there some kind of spark between Cate and Rand? Was there more than professional suspicion and outright dislike happening?

A shiver ran through her.

Time to get herself together. Rand and his effect on her was not something she should spend time pondering. She had her father and three kids to worry about. Three kids who mattered.

Three kids she wasn't about to start leaving now. When they were younger, they'd been willing to help her at the day care. Not so much anymore. But they still needed someone to run herd over them at all times.

On the other hand, she couldn't see how she could

stand to not spend all her free time at Dad's bedside. She'd have to figure out something before school let out that afternoon.

And then there was the daycare.

She sighed on her way upstairs to Lindsay's room. "It's time to take a big-girl pill—for both of us."

THREE

Telling Mr. and Mrs. Tucker about the fire and Wilma's injuries proved harder than Rand had expected. But he'd gotten through it, holding Mr. Tucker's frail hand, hugging Mrs. Tucker while she sobbed.

The one thing he'd left out of his retelling was, in his opinion, the most important detail. At this point, neither one of them could have handled knowing the basement of their theater had been co-opted for the production of methamphetamine.

Worse yet, they would never be able to handle the possibility of Wilma cooking the meth.

The Tuckers' only daughter had always been a true eccentric, but drugs? Had Wilma changed that much while she'd been away from Loganton?

Evidence pointed to her. She had the access, and her parents' care at the Pines cost plenty, not to mention all the money she'd sunk into the renovations at the theater. Drugs made quick cash.

Rand rubbed his eyes as he stared at the morning news on TV. He needed sleep, but he also needed to wind down before he stood a chance of nodding off.

What a night.

He'd taken the weekend off. Scotty Woodburn, a buddy from the fire department in Charlotte, had married his latest girlfriend on Saturday. Rand had gone to the wedding—Scotty's third—and come home about an hour and a half before the call from the firehouse had come in.

When his cell phone buzzed, he'd looked out his bedroom window to see the orange glow rising from somewhere on Main Street. He'd jumped in his car and hurried over.

The last thing he'd expected to find was Cate Caldwell, looking more appealing than he ever thought possible, at the scene of a fire in Loganton.

She'd been a year or two behind him in school and they hadn't had a lot in common. Her rebellious behavior and crazy stunts, however, had made her known to everyone in town. And that horrible Thanksgiving weekend when her sister and his cousin were killed would always be etched in his memory.

Rand had been the newest rookie at the fire station back then and while he'd never wanted a fire to break out, he had been looking forward to the chance to serve. His first call had been to that vehicle fire. He went through all the steps—donning his gear, hopping on the engine truck. The adrenaline pumped through his veins, while his youthful idealism reached its peak.

He'd never forget the sight of Ross's van just feet away from the Caldwell driveway, the flames devouring everything they touched.

Across the road, two teens had stared at the devastation. Cate Caldwell's purple Mohawk had been singed, and she'd held her infant niece in her arms, the two-year-old twin boys on either side of her. Her horror had seemed incongruous with all the studs in her pierced nostril, lip, eyebrows and ears.

To Rand, her whimpers had sounded weak in the face of her mother and father's stark grief. Their sobs had echoed in the icy, silent dusk.

Cate had been dating Sam Burns, a kid known to have substance issues. After another argument with Joe, the two punk lovebirds had left the Caldwell house, on their way to yet another party. Mandy and Ross had been on their way home to the Caldwell's place, where they'd been living while their home underwent renovation, after they'd enjoyed Thanksgiving dinner with Ross's parents.

Sam had already had too much to drink. The kid should never have been behind the wheel of a car. Ross had swerved to avoid the inebriated teen and his van had hit an icy patch. The van struck a brick wall, which had crashed down on the front seat, killing the adults.

Only the children, strapped in their car seats in the back, had survived. Cate had had the wherewithal to go in and rescue them. By the time she was done, flames had engulfed the van.

Rand wasn't sure why Cate had made such an impression on him that day. Maybe it had to do with the ludicrous contrast between the stark tragedy and the silly vanity of those piercings. The thought of all those holes had always made Rand cringe.

On top of everything else, she'd worn solid black, strategically torn and bedecked with large safety pins, carabiner clips and even the odd piece of gray duct tape here and there. She'd been quite the sight.

· The Cate he'd found in the middle of Main Street a handful of hours ago had been far more approachable, softer—appealing, even. Fear for her father's life had shown in her tense posture, the tight line of her lips, the edgy way her eyes darted from place to place, seeking, looking for anything that might bolster her hope.

Her hair had tumbled around her face to her shoulders in a tangle of tawny waves and he'd found himself wanting to ease it off her forehead, to touch it and see if it was as silky as it looked.

And Cate's clothes? Well, it seemed she still chose to go the unconventional route. It was, though, entirely possible she liked to sleep in the college basketball T-shirt and blue plaid pants she'd worn. She might have been in bed when Neal called.

The urge to find out if she'd changed in the years since that horrible day caught him by surprise. He'd heard she had. But was she still skating on the edge of danger? Flirting with prosecution? Giving her poor father nightmares and ulcers? Rand hadn't been home long enough to know.

Before he had the chance to examine his curiosity, the phone rang. Despite his exhaustion, he answered.

"Hey, stranger," Sheriff Hal Benson said. "How long have you been back? A month? Six weeks? I'm feeling neglected here. A call would've been welcome."

Rand chuckled. "Not from what I hear. Newlyweds don't often want an old friend butting into their bliss."

"Yeah, well. This old friend has time for Rand Mason. But I'm calling for professional reasons, actually."

"Go ahead and shoot. Don't know if I'll have the answers you want, but I'll try."

He heard Hal's rough inhale. "I don't have questions as much as a favor to ask."

A touch of excitement unfurled in the pit of Rand's stomach. "Go for it."

"Joe Caldwell said he found the remains of a meth lab in the theater basement. Looks like the stuff exploded. In the last couple of years we've put away one dealer and prosecuted his accomplice, but we've also racked up a couple of deaths. We haven't been able to put them out of business. As soon as we shut them down in one place, they pop up in another."

Rand knew what was coming. Half of him couldn't wait to dig into a fresh arson investigation. The other half feared the effect another dive into the pits of the underworld might have on his humanity, especially because this case touched on the lives of folks that mattered to him. "Sounds about right."

"I'm pretty sure we're dealing with more than home-grown opportunists here. Someone somewhere is calling the shots. You've followed more than one arsonist to his organized crime pals. We need your experience if we're going to have any chance at getting more than just the guy who calls the shots here— starting with last night's fire, which I'm sure is already sitting on your plate. We'll get further much quicker if we join forces and we might catch more than the random meth cooker, which is all we've done so far. Will you give us a hand? Cross-agency cooperation?"

After years as an arson investigator, he'd come back to Loganton to get away from this very thing. He'd been looking to put out fires and help keep the folks in Loganton safe. That was it. But now…

Now things had changed. And Rand did want to work with Hal Benson, who'd just been reelected as county sheriff, to try and catch the mastermind behind the lab, to put them out of business permanently.

It might soothe his battered soul to mingle with the good guys for a while, rather than just muck around, undercover, where the bad guys roamed 24/7.

And yet, he couldn't deny that certain hesitation, that touch of reluctance. Why was he so torn? What was holding him back?

He ran a hand through his hair, irritated with his double-mindedness. Sure, he knew his darkest fear. He didn't want to learn he'd lost his ability to empathize, that he'd turned into a robotic investigator, the kind of man he'd watched other arson investigators become.

A man like Scotty, who kept others at arm's length, and went through women like most men did cars.

But he wanted to find out who was behind all this, even if it was Wilma—or Cate. Or maybe he just wanted the opportunity to see Cate again. Regardless, he needed to do this.

Rand sat up tall in his dad's old recliner. He would just have to believe his concern meant all wasn't lost. Yet.

"Sure," he said. "How can I help?"

Cate grabbed her purse and car keys. "Come on, you guys! We've got to get to school and we're running way late."

Lindsay left the kitchen and slipped by her on the way to the car. The boys continued to drag their feet.

"I have soccer practice after school," Tommy said. "But I can't find my cleats."

"Anybody see my math homework?" Robby asked. "I can't find it. And I did it—every last dumb problem."

Cate looked around in search of the elusive homework. "Cleats are in the laundry room. After your last game, they had more mud on them than our flower beds, so I scraped them clean for you." When she saw nothing that might resemble the missing assignment in the kitchen, she headed for the dining room, where she found the AWOL homework under the china hutch.

With her patience stretched to its utmost, Cate eventually herded everyone into the car. Phone calls to the nurses' station didn't satisfy—she wanted to get to her father's side and see him herself as soon as possible.

The drive to the elementary school took less than ten minutes. Once she'd delivered the kids to the halls of academia, she raced to the hospital.

She ran into the lobby, the shoulders of her white shirt damp from the drippy braid that swung from side to side each time she turned her head. Who cared what her hair looked like when Dad was in the ICU and the kids were, well, their usual, challenging selves?

As Cate approached the elevators, a woman called out her name. "Your dad's up in surgery right now. To reset his leg. You might want to go wait in the OR unit's family lounge. Let one of the nurses up there know where you are, and Doc Shields will come tell you how everything went once they're done."

Cate thanked the hospital administrator and slipped inside the elevator, punching the appropriate button. She stopped by the nurses' station, gave them her name, grabbed a cup of coffee and eyed the comfortable-looking armchair in the far corner of the waiting room. A long swig of the hot, strong brew warmed its way down her middle.

"How's he doing?"

She gulped, blinked and set the coffee down on the side table by her seat. "Rand. I didn't see you when I walked in."

He dropped down into the chair next to hers. "I just got here. Wilma's about to go into surgery and her parents wanted to see her. I drove them over. Thought I'd hang around until she comes out."

"That's nice of you. How's she doing?"

"Considering a portion of the balcony collapsed on her and your dad, I think she's doing great—both of them, actually. Joe's in surgery, too?"

"They're setting his leg. It looks like they'll have to use a metal plate. He's going to be the Bionic Man when he leaves here."

"I'm glad to hear he's well enough for surgery."

The image of the flames leaping to the black sky flashed behind her eyes. Cate shuddered. "Me, too."

Just then, police chief Ethan Rodgers and sheriff Hal Benson walked into the waiting room. They headed straight for Cate and Rand.

"'Morning," the chief said. "Mind if we ask you a couple of questions?"

Cate looked from one newcomer to the other, then to Rand and finally back to the chief. "You mean me?"

The chief nodded. "We'd like you to tell us what your father said in the ambulance last night."

"Not much. He told us he'd found a meth lab in the basement of the theater."

"That's it?" Disappointment rang in Rand's voice.

"He also said something about an explosion. But that's it."

The three men exchanged looks.

"An explosion means it might have been accidental," Ethan said. "But we do have a witness. She says she saw someone at the side entrance after the film let out."

Cate frowned. "Then that wouldn't mean an accident."

"Not necessarily," Rand answered. "If they set fire to the lab, it could have exploded, too. Meth requires enough flammable material to blow a building to bits."

Hal Benson looked from one to the other. "The question here is whether the person this witness saw was at the theater or just a passerby. Did they burn the place to erase evidence? Or did the meth just explode?"

"In either case, it means they hadn't abandoned the lab," Rand added. "The one who torched it—if it was torched—might still be around. We stand a chance of catching them."

Cate stared but read nothing in his neutral expression. "We? I thought I'd heard you'd come back to sell books—when you weren't putting out fires, that is."

He shrugged. "Maybe."

Confusion didn't come close to describing her state of mind. "Are things so bad in Loganton that we need both the DEA and an arson investigator here?"

"Retired," Ethan said. "Saw too much, got too banged up. It was time to get myself a whole new life. So here I am, new job, new wife, new life. I'm a happy man."

Rand nodded. "Me, too—sort of. Minus the wife, of course."

"Back to your question," Hal inserted. "They're much welcome here. We have crimes to solve. Of all kinds." He waved toward Cate. "How're you feeling? How's your head?"

She dismissed his question with a careless wave. "I'm fine. But it sounds as though my town might not be."

"We can handle whatever comes our way," Hal answered. "But we'll never turn down help. And you guys are always willing to help, right, Rand? Ethan?" The sheriff waited for Rand's nod. "We can't let this stuff snag any more of our kids. Think about it, Cate. You have Mandy's three to raise. Do you want a meth lab in their hometown?"

The screech of tires burned again in her memory. She closed her eyes and saw Mandy and Ross's van feet away from Sam's car. She heard the crash, the cries, saw the mangled metal and the crumbled brick wall.

Substance abuse had ravaged her life. She knew the destruction it brought. Nausea threatened, but with a prayer for strength, she brought herself under control. She forced her eyes open and found Rand staring at her.

"What?" she said. "What aren't you telling me?"

Again, the three men looked at each other. After the briefest nod to the other two, Rand leaned toward her.

"During his first go-through at the scene, Neal

Hunter made a discovery in that basement. He found a body in the meth lab. We're waiting for an ID."

Cate drove to the day care center once her father had gone back to the ICU after surgery, her thoughts in a whirl, her nerves knotted.

She'd had a chance to see him, but the nurses had chased her out when he'd started to fade. She would have been happy to stay by his side, just to keep him company as he slept, but she knew how strict rules were in the unit. Family members were allowed to visit only for limited periods of time throughout the day. She planned to take the kids to see him after school let out.

Now she had to deal with Mrs. Washburn and the day care. As if it were a normal day.

But nothing could change reality. A fire had consumed a historic building, injured her father and Wilma and evidently killed a drug dealer. Nothing was normal anymore.

She didn't feel normal. Fear kept trying to take root, but another, more potent feeling nudged it aside. Cate needed to know who had been behind the lab, the fire and Dad's and Wilma's injuries.

Not only did she need to know, but she also needed to see that person behind bars and the drug banished from town.

Her experience years ago gave her a certain level of insight, of urgency. She hoped others agreed.

At Cate's Cozy Corner, she walked in to a chorus of greetings. The kids always made her feel needed and she loved to make them smile. As she peeled one crumb-crusher after another off her legs, she communicated with Dena by means of head bobs and eyebrow waggles.

Geri Harwood, another of Cate's teachers, snagged the next munchkin intent on latching onto Cate's legs. "You and Dena go on. I'll keep the natives from getting too restless."

"We won't be long." She felt so blessed, being able to count on her terrific employees.

Dena waited only long enough for Cate to close her office door. "What's up?"

Cate propped a hip on her desk. "Way, way too much. As far as Dad's concerned, it's going to be a long haul. And I'm going to be out more than in. We're going to need to hire additional help."

"Do you want me to contact that agency you used to find Geri?"

She tried to smile. "Are we twins separated at birth?"

Dena laughed. "No, but I've worked for you since you set up shop. I think I know what we need around here." She put on a mock stern glare. "And if you'd only quit being such a control freak, Boss Lady, I could help you carry some of that stress you haul around with you. You know. A burden shared, and all that."

"I'm not stressed—"

"Wanna try that one again? I've never known you to tell a fib."

"Well, I've never felt stressed. At least, not until this morning."

Dena drew her glasses down her nose and peered at Cate over the rims. "How about those headaches you keep getting? And let me tell ya, that bottle of antacids on your bookshelf is not a decorative statement."

"Everyone gets headaches and heartburn."

"Yeah, but not constantly and not while virtually killing herself to prove all the gossips in town wrong."

"I'm not doing that…am I?"

"Sure looks like it from where I'm standing."

Was Dena right? Was Cate still fighting that old battle? Hadn't she been able to forgive and move forward? What was she trying to prove? And to whom?

Well, the gossip had bothered her. And even though she hadn't done so intentionally, she supposed she had doubled her efforts and worked to prove them wrong. She wanted to do right by the kids.

Cate sighed. This wasn't the time to worry about that. She'd have to pray about it later. "Okay, Wise One. I'll think about it and get back to you some other time. Right now, I have bigger things to think about."

"Like your dad and the kids."

Cate gestured toward the playroom. "And you guys— these kids and the three of you. I've got to figure out how I'm going to juggle everything, plus help Dad—"

The phone rang, interrupting Cate. She picked up. "Hello?"

"Cate? It's Rand. I just got a call from Hal Benson. Remember the body they found in the basement of the theater?"

"As if I could have forgotten." She mouthed a request for Dena to give her a minute and then sat in her desk chair.

No way was this a courtesy call.

After a few seconds of silence, Rand went on. "I realize it might seem strange for me to call you, but we feel you need to know."

"Me?" A shiver ran up her back. "What exactly do you feel I need to know?"

"We just finished searching the scene. We found a photo album of yours in the basement. With the corpse's belongings."

FOUR

"Album? What album?"

"Your photo album lay right next to the body," Rand repeated.

"I really don't know what you're talking about. I'm not missing a photo album." He heard her take a deep breath. "And who is it that died?"

Hmm…she sounded confused. What was going on? Did she really not know about the album? "We don't know yet. The body was too burned to ID at the scene. We're waiting for an autopsy and probably even DNA testing to see who we're dealing with."

"So why would you say the album's mine?"

"Because your name's on the inside cover, and most of the photos are of you and a bunch of…your school friends."

Cate paused at his references to her past and there was a brief, tense silence. Maybe he had come on a bit too strong, too judgmental. Even though they both knew she had nothing to brag about in that department, she probably didn't need the constant reminders, much less an accusing tone of voice on his part. He'd have to rein himself in, be the professional he took pride in being.

She cleared her throat. "But I'm not missing any album, so I can't imagine—"

"Trust me. There's no way we could be mistaken. You were *unique* back then, and there's no doubt it's your name in the book."

"You'll understand if I ask to see it, right?"

He considered her request for a moment. "Fine. I'll show you the album. Since I'm going to have questions for you, and the phone's not the best way to handle this, why don't we set up a meeting? I don't think you want me to come over while your niece and nephews are around, any more than I figure you want to answer me while you're at work."

"I appreciate your thoughtfulness. How about we meet at Granny Annie's Diner in about twenty minutes? I have time now to grab lunch and talk before I need to pick up the kids at school."

"I'll be there."

As he gathered the album and left his office, Rand fought down the twinges of…what was it? He'd never felt anything like it before. He couldn't quite call it excitement. He was investigating a fire—and a death—after all. Not exactly a fun experience. But then again, he couldn't stop the image of Cate from bursting into his thoughts every few minutes.

He couldn't deny it. He was looking forward to seeing her again. He wanted to see her reaction to the album. He wanted to see if she really seemed as surprised by it as she'd said. He hoped she was.

But what if she was some great actress? What if she

turned out to be implicated in the meth lab? The fire? What would her guilt do to Joe? The twins and Lindsay?

A sick sense swam into his gut. Cate being guilty would destroy Joe.

And as much as the thought of her possible guilt disgusted Rand deep in his gut, that same gut kept telling him she was as innocent as she said. Why couldn't he just accept his instincts, as he'd done in so many other investigations? Was it all about Cate?

Did he want her to be innocent because…well, because she was so attractive? Because he felt such a strong pull between them? Was he willing to consider that kind of relationship with Cate Caldwell?

He slammed the door to his silver SUV and turned the key in the ignition.

No way. He wasn't ready to see Cate in that way. She was part of an investigation. And that was how he had to keep thinking of her. Period.

End of story.

On arriving, Rand tucked the album under his arm, and walked into Granny Annie's Diner, a true fixture in Loganville. The moist warmth of the eatery, redolent of spices and roasting meats, made him think of family dinners and his aunts' hugs when he stepped inside the front door. With nods and waves he greeted the regulars who called out his name as he walked down the main aisle. Granny Annie whooped when she saw him.

"Got me a fresh, new meatloaf just outta the oven here, Captain. Want me to make you up a platter?"

"Give me a couple of minutes. I'm meeting someone."

"Just give me a holler, and I'll serve you myself."

One could always count on Granny. With a sweeping glance, he spotted an empty booth at the end of the left-hand row.

The diner door opened just as the older woman was disappearing into her domain, and Cate walked in. She greeted the proprietress, and then hurried down to meet Rand, Granny at her heels, order pad in the wrinkled hand.

"That meatloaf's still waiting," Granny said. "But so's a super lasagna."

Rand laughed. "You know me too well. Bring on the meatloaf, and don't go stingy with the gravy, either."

"Drowning, my man." The older woman winked. "It'll come drowning in the stuff, just the way you like it."

"Same here," Cate said, then slid deeper into the corner of the booth. "I see we're both fans of Granny's meatloaf."

"Is there any better?"

"Haven't found it yet."

He waved vaguely. "There you have it. I found nothing like it while I was gone."

After a brief, polite silence, Cate asked him what he thought of the changes the town had undergone since he'd left all those years ago.

"To someone who's been away, they're minor. Sure, I saw the new planters, the added age to the buildings on Main Street, and the two others that were built to replace the ones demolished. But it's still Loganton—home."

Granny zipped up to their table, white crockery plates piled high with fragrant food. "Enjoy!"

"Thanks!" Cate said.

Rand drew in an appreciative breath. "I intend to do just that."

They ate for a couple of silent minutes, then Cate glanced up again. "Do you miss the excitement of your former career?"

Excitement? Stress and tension were more like it. But he wasn't going to go into those details. Not with her. She might ask why he'd left in the first place, and he didn't want to revisit the accident that had affected both their lives. Instead, he focused on the present.

"How are the twins doing in school?" he asked. "They strike me as a handful."

She arched a brow at his question-to-a-question answer, but went ahead and told him about Tommy and Robby's fascination with bugs and rodents, and both boys' talents on the soccer field.

A couple more attempts on her part to carry on a conversation gave a superficial sense of calm to the meal, but Rand couldn't help noticing the nervous edginess she maintained the whole time. He realized it couldn't be easy for her to eat with him. Besides, he'd heard many fire victims say how their lives took on a nightmarish, surreal quality after the event. On top of all that, because of what they'd found during their investigation of the basement, Cate's father's precarious condition wasn't the only thing that could affect her and hers. The album…what would that discovery do to the present she seemed to have worked so hard to build on the ashes of her past?

While Rand would have expected her to feel like hiding from the painful memories and the many mistakes she'd made all those years ago, she'd gone to school, and then come home to the town full of memories. It seemed that over time she'd grown to where she preferred to face troubles head-on rather than dodge them. He had to admire that kind of guts.

Meals finished, he felt as ready to deal with whatever he was about to learn as he ever would be. And then he'd help Joe cope with the fallout.

He put down his napkin seconds after she did, but before he could ask his first question, she hit him with one of her own.

"Who's the witness?"

"Can't tell you. You know that—it's an ongoing investigation."

"But I'm not the usual Jane-on-the-street. That's my father who almost died."

"I still can't tell you."

She looked frustrated and there was nothing he could do about it. He wondered how her answers to his questions would strike him. The album—which she had yet to see—put her in a bad position. Well, there was nothing much she was going to say about it, not until he produced the book.

He studied her for a few more seconds than gave a nod. He dipped his hand below the tabletop to the bench at his side, and then brought up the ziplock plastic bag, its contents charred. "Take a look."

Being right didn't feel all that great, especially when Rand saw her wince as she caught a glimpse of the burnt item. A pained expression distorted her pretty features. She remembered the album.

She took a deep breath. "You were right. It was mine. But I haven't seen it in years. Can't even remember the last time I saw it…sometime shortly before Mandy and Ross died." She shuddered. "But it doesn't matter. I wouldn't have wanted to see it, no matter what. The memories—" She closed her eyes. "I don't go out of my way to find reminders of how my stupidity led to the loss of two wonderful lives."

He studied her for a moment, then surprise struck him. Grief and remorse. How unexpected…in the Cate he remembered. But, as she said, this was a new Cate. "You're still beating yourself up about those deaths, aren't you?"

She tipped her head and met his gaze. "I was the one who insisted on dating Sam. I knew what he was, but I found his flaws an irresistible lure, and don't ask me why, because I don't know. All I can say is that danger equaled excitement, and Sam got a rise out of Mom and Dad—two pluses. That rebellious conflict cost us a huge part of our family."

He weighed her response. So the teenaged flake had developed some depth. Unexpected though the discovery was, he found it appealing. Contrition went a long way. Even if she might be carrying it a bit far. He rapped the table with his knuckles, looked up and met her gaze. He sighed. "Sam's the one who chose to drink, Cate. You had nothing to do with that."

Surprise widened Cate's eyes. "Look, I'm the one who chose to go out with him. And I know it."

A wave of tenderness swept over him at her admission of responsibility. He felt the urge to cover her hand with his, but he refrained. This was business, not a date.

Or was it?

He shook himself and got right back to his point.

"That still didn't relieve him of the responsibility to drive sober. You were sober. I remember reading the newspaper reports. It surprised a lot of people when your blood alcohol level came back at zip."

"Don't go making me out to be more righteous than I was. Back then I joined in on the drinking often enough. I was clean that day because he'd just picked me up."

Again, admiration tried to rise. He fought to keep it at bay. "But you never developed a problem."

She gave him a wry grin. "Not for any abundance of virtue."

He fell silent again, staring at the coffee spoon he'd picked up. "Sounds to me as though you're still wearing a coat of borrowed guilt. You might want to return it to its rightful owner."

Cate tipped up her chin. "I take responsibility for my actions. And I did spend some years back then rebelling in the worst way. It's only by God's unending grace that I didn't end up either needing serious rehab or in a morgue."

"That's a stark self-evaluation."

"It's a realistic assessment of my sins."

"Sin…" He shook his head. "Don't know much about sin. I think it's more a matter of bad choices."

"Wrong choices made while I knew what God expected of me. Sounds like plain-vanilla sin to me."

He stirred the dregs of his coffee with the spoon. "I'm sure you remember what's in those pictures—lots of them feature you and Sam. Have you heard from him lately?"

Cate shrugged. "Last time I talked to him was

seconds before the accident. I never said a word to him after that. I had nothing to say."

He tapped the table in a dull rhythm. Then he met her gaze. "No contact at all, huh?"

She leaned forward. "You have to understand where I'm coming from. I turned my back on everything I did that hurt my God, my family and myself the night my sister died. I wanted no contact with Sam after that. I've made something of my life in the years since. I'm not the same person I once was. I'd never have anything to do with a meth lab."

"I didn't say—"

"You didn't have to." She stood and slipped her purse onto her shoulder. "Your questions did all the talking for you. But come on. You don't really think I left that album in the basement of the theater, do you?"

Something deep within him urged him to set her mind at ease, to reassure her. But he couldn't. He didn't have the evidence to clear her. Regardless what his gut was telling him.

When he didn't respond, fear crossed her face. Then she squared her shoulders and met his gaze. "Well, Rand—Captain Mason, let me assure you I had nothing to do with the lab or the fire. And I have no idea how the album wound up where it did. Now, if you don't mind, I have to go to the hospital. I'd rather spend my days watching my dad sleep than rehashing the worst time of my life. I hope the album helps you figure out what happened. Keep it. I sure don't want it."

"I have to keep it, Cate. It's evidence in what probably is a murder."

She shivered visibly. "A murder I didn't commit."

* * *

Without giving Rand a chance to respond, she went to the register, paid and left. In her car, she tamped down her temper, prayed for calm, wisdom, discernment—peace, more than anything else, deep and abiding peace in spite of the situation.

She couldn't really blame him for his questions. They'd been valid. It wasn't his fault they'd hit her sweet spot.

In junior high, she became aware that drugs had come to Loganton, but at that time, only the outcasts were using. Then she went to high school. And met Sam.

In recent years, the town had seen a couple of busts and even some drug-related deaths. From the vantage point of a responsible aunt helping to raise three kids, she'd worried about it. She couldn't stand the thought of any of that poison coming near one of her late-sister's precious kids.

Cate shuddered and pressed her forehead against the steering wheel. She'd felt compelled to do something about the situation, but she hadn't known exactly what. A few months ago, after a drug bust in town, she'd received an unexpected offer, one that had planted a seed in her heart. If she accepted, it would mean she would have to take on even more responsibility than she already carried, but when the offer was made, she'd figured she'd have time to prepare. Now, as a parent— she'd effectively become one, thanks to the fire at the theater—she couldn't stand by and let drugs continue to creep into Loganton. Not anymore.

She turned the key in the ignition then pulled out of the diner's parking lot, headed for the high school.

Once there, she walked across the almost-full parking lot to the massive glass front doors.

She buzzed and identified herself to the administration's secretary, who moments later told her the man she'd come to see was due back in his office at any minute. Willing to wait, Cate walked down the empty hall, accompanied by the hushed murmur of teachers and students behind closed classrooms. She paused before a gleaming oak door, then sat in a nearby chair in the hall.

Alec Hollinger, Loganton High's guidance counselor, and his wife Beth, had moved into the house next door two years earlier. Since then, he'd turned the school's guidance and career department on its ear, doubled the number of graduates headed for college, become a member of the church, taken over its high school youth group leadership with his wife's help, and had participated in the congregation's many activities. The couple had also joined Cate, her dad, and the kids for numerous backyard soccer games and various barbecues.

Then he'd asked Cate to consider helping him with the teens at church once his pregnant wife delivered the triplets she carried. Four weeks ago, however, Beth was admitted to a hospital in Charlotte due to complications. During the Hollingers' tenure, the group had grown enough that Alec had split the kids into girls and guys for the sake of better management and more one-on-one ministry.

In light of her own misguided adolescence, Cate had been tempted by the opportunity to help lead the girls because she now wished someone more youth-savvy had been at the helm of the teen group when she'd needed help. But she feared taking on even more responsibility than she already bore. She'd prayed many times over her decision. If she failed in any of her roles, she'd never be able to live with herself.

Now, after the fire and the subsequent revelations, she also knew she'd never live with herself if she failed to step out in faith and answer the Lord's call.

She believed the mess she'd made of her teen years uniquely qualified her to speak against the ills of substance abuse. Could this be God's way of redeeming that wasted time? Was God using Cate's rebellion for good?

Footsteps echoed nearer. Cate drew a calming breath. She'd made up her mind. A man appeared at the end of the hallway, striding toward her. She stood. "Hey."

The blond guidance counselor stopped. "Cate! I'm surprised to see you here. Is there a problem?"

"I have a decision for you, Alec. If you still want a temporary partner for the youth group, you just got one. When do you want me to start?"

On Tuesday, Cate felt jumpy, nervous and no matter where she went or what she did, she couldn't shake the vague feeling someone was watching. She didn't know why she felt that way and she hadn't noticed anything unusual around her, but the sensation remained.

Time after time the small hairs at the back of her neck rose, her awareness at its highest level.

She asked herself a million times why she was so nervous, but she came up with no concrete reason. Had Rand's suspicion made her paranoid? She couldn't really take it too seriously. After all, she'd had nothing to do with the lab or the fire. As he'd figure out soon enough.

Still, his doubts loomed large in her thoughts. As did the weird sensation.

Was someone really there?

The only person who came to mind was the person who had attacked her at the theater. But that would mean it hadn't been a random act, which was something she'd tried very hard to believe.

As much as the possibility scared her, she couldn't spend her day dwelling on it. So with extra vigilance, she went ahead with her plans and spent the day with her dad.

The fire chief remained weak from his injuries and medical personnel hovered. Cate couldn't complain because she was doing the same. At a quarter to three, she leaned over the steel railing and pressed a kiss to his lean cheek. At the feel of his unshaven skin against her face, tears welled. As a little girl, she'd rubbed her hand against the stubble and giggled at the sensation. Dad had always loved the game.

Lindsay played it these days.

He had to recover. Lindsay needed her gramps.

"See ya later," she whispered.

A deep sigh escaped his lips, but the pain medications had done their job. He was out for the count.

Cate headed home to meet the kids at the bus stop. She wasn't sure what she was going to do to keep them busy. It wouldn't do anybody any good for them to focus on the hole Dad's absence left in their midst.

As usual, the twins were going at it when they climbed into the van.

"'Let *me* help you, Mrs. Washburn,'" Robby singsonged. "'I so *looooove* to be the suck-up of the *whoooooole* class.'"

"Just shut up, bird-breath. You don't know how to be nice. You just think you know everything."

"Suck-up!"

"Know-nothing!"

Cate stuck two fingers in the corners of her mouth and let out a shrill whistle. The boys piped down.

A tiny tug came at the sleeve of her blouse. "Hi, Aunt Catey," Lindsay said, her voice barely over a whisper. "I had brownies, 'cause it was Bethany's birthday."

Cate gave her niece a quick hug. "That's great, honey. I'm so glad." Then, with a stern frown, she faced the twins. "Next time one of you says something impolite to the other, I'm going to charge you the victim's allowance."

She started the van and out the corner of her eye, saw Tommy scratch his head. "Huh?"

The rearview mirror displayed Robby's jutted chin. "Whaddaya mean, 'charge the victim's allowance'?"

She checked to see that all three seat belts were fastened, then pulled away from the curb. "That, dear darlings, means that the one who does the insulting will be turning his allowance back to me. In turn, I'll pay damages to the one who was wronged."

She heard twin gulps. Peace reigned during the ride home.

"Chores first," she called as they all bounded out of the vehicle before she even withdrew the key from the ignition. "Then homework. If you guys get everything done—and done well—I could be persuaded to order pizza."

"Woo-hoo!"

"All right!"

Lindsay paused, turned and smiled at Cate. "My favorite, please? Pepperoni, right?"

"I'll order three—one plain, one pepperoni and one meatball. That way, the boys can have—" she shuddered "—breakfast pizza."

"Yuck!" The little girl headed toward the house.

Before following the kids, Cate scooped the mail from the box and to her surprise, found a package addressed to her.

As always, she went into the living room and collapsed into her dad's armchair. She sorted out the junk mail and her stack shrank down to only the package, two utilities and the phone bill. She set the boring stuff aside and tore into the brown envelope.

When it gave way, Cate was left holding a fistful of photos and a folded sheet of notebook paper. She also had a throbbing head, a pounding chest and a roiling stomach.

While she wanted to look away, she found she couldn't. She stared with fascinated horror. The last time she'd seen those pictures was the day before the accident that took her sister's life. A handful of newspaper clippings—her college graduation announcement, the Goings and Comings column note of her return to town, the announcement of the opening of her day care—slipped out from the folded page.

She'd never given these old photos of her and Sam a thought over the years—just like the charred album.

With trembling fingers, she unfolded the page torn from a spiral-bound notebook and began to read. As she did, the words swam before her, their meaning full of danger and threat. Fear gripped her and she gasped for breath.

While she knew it was crazy, she again felt as though someone was watching her. She stood, hurried to the front door, threw the deadbolt and then ran to the kitchen to do the same to the back door.

With considerable strength of will, she made herself read the message again.

I'm so sorry I couldn't return these to you sooner or in person even now. But you know they were all I had of you. They kept me company in my cell and helped my love stay strong. I've always known we belong together, that we'll be together again soon. Now that I'm out, you know it won't be long. You'll see. I'm putting together a deal that'll set us up for life. When it's all set, I'll come for you and we can go away together. I've always been yours, just as you've always been mine. I'm so glad you waited for me, but now you won't have to wait much longer. Knowing you were there is what kept me going all these years. We belong together. Forever. Soon, Cate, very soon, I'll never let you go again.

Yours,

Sam

Was Sam the one she'd felt watching her? If so, she had reason to worry. The letter revealed something very wrong with Sam's mental state. How he could think she'd ever want to see him again was beyond her.

"Aunt Catey!" Tommy wailed. "Hurry up here. Lindsay just barfed birthday brownies all over my school shoes."

"You dweeb!" Robby bellowed. "You never finished cleaning the bathtub and the water's overflowed all over the bathroom floor."

"Aunt Cate," Lindsay cried, "I'm sick!"

Cate told herself to shut her mind to any further thought of Sam Burns and his horrifying letter. She'd deal with it once her niece felt well again.

Easier said than done. Would she ever get beyond Sam and her past?

Wednesday night, instead of heading for the single women's Bible study after she'd settled the twins and Lindsay in their classrooms, Cate followed Alec to the new youth building at the rear of the church property. The congregation had recently dedicated the structure, which still smelled of fresh paint.

Alec slapped his hand flat against the huge steel door. "Ready?"

"I better be, right?"

"Teens eat wimps for breakfast, you know."

"Better than most. I was one of those wimp-eating teens." She closed her eyes and said a quick prayer. "Let's go."

Music, giggles and rumbly guffaws hit Cate's ears as she and Alec stepped inside the gym. The thump-thump-thump of basketballs provided a rhythmic downbeat to the overall cacophony.

"Yo!" the tallest basketball player called out. "Mr. Alec's here."

When the cavernous room fell silent, Alec waved toward Cate. "I've got news—especially for the girls. Beth and the triplets are still hanging in there at the hospital, but she misses you and says hi." When greetings for his bedridden wife died down, he went on. "This is Cate Caldwell and she's going to help me with the girls for a while."

Polite clapping greeted his announcement.

Alec went on. "Before we break out into groups, let's pray. Any special requests?"

A list of teen concerns dribbled out. The kids' openness impressed Cate. At their age, she never would have revealed her inner self like that.

But she had learned. "If you guys don't mind, I'd appreciate prayer for my dad and Miss Wilma Tucker. Y'all know about the fire at the theater. They were hurt and are in stable but critical condition at the hospital."

The teens' compassion encouraged Cate to go on. "Miss Wilma's also going to have some pretty serious bills once she recovers. She'll have medical bills on top of all that money she borrowed to restore the theater. Let's pray about that, too, okay?"

A sassy blonde with glamour-gal eye makeup rose to her knees and waved a hand.

Alec acknowledged her. "What's up, Hillary?"

"You know how scripture says faith without works is not so good? How about we do something to help? That'd be putting our faith to work, right?"

Cate recognized leadership when it jumped up in front of her. "What would you suggest?"

Bake sales, coupon books and car washes were dismissed right away. Nick, the basketball giant, pinned Cate with a perceptive stare. "Everyone goes to the movies, right? I think whatever we do has to come from the whole town."

Cate drew her brows together. "Isn't that a tall order?"

He shrugged. "Look at the Fall Fest. Everyone does something and it works. We should do something like that."

Hillary high-fived him. Chatter broke out again.

Cate looked at her watch and turned to Alec. "What about tonight's Bible study?"

"You kidding? I want to see where this leads."

It led to the creation of the town's first, and hopefully only, Tuckerpalooza. Since Christmas was fast approaching, the teens wanted to capitalize on the season's feelings of generosity. They planned the event for the lull between Christmas and New Year's.

Hillary waved. "Let's keep things at five bucks or less."

Marly Wooten, a quiet teen in Hillary's shadow, stood. "How about if we have people sign up for blessings?"

Alec leaned his elbows on his knees. "Blessings? What do you mean?"

The redhead blushed. "Stuff like taking Mr. and Mrs. Tucker to the doctor, cleaning Miss Wilma's apartment, rebuilding the theater. All that has to happen, even while Miss Wilma is in the hospital. If people do it, they'll bless the Tuckers and the money we raise doesn't have to pay for it."

"Faith in action," Cate murmured and Alec grinned.

The group broke off into its two sections and Cate worked to get to know her girls. Too soon, it was time to go.

And then Cate's niece and nephews ran into the gym. She'd hoped to go over details for the benefit with Alec, but had to postpone. She apologized.

"No problem," he said. "Go on home. I miss Beth's

cooking, so some of your cinnamon rolls on Saturday morning would work for me. We can brainstorm then."

"You're on," she laughed. "See ya Saturday."

Still laughing, she herded Lindsay and the twins toward the door. That's when she noticed Marly at the front window, her gaze fixed on the darkness outside, anxiety on her face.

The girl started when Cate placed a hand on her shoulder. "I'm sorry, Marly. I didn't mean to startle you. Are you all right?"

Lightly freckled cheeks colored with a faint blush. Marly shrugged. "I suppose."

"Are you waiting for someone?"

Another shrug. "My mom had to show a house tonight. She thought she'd make it back here in time. Those nights when she doesn't, I catch a ride with one of the other kids."

Cate peered outside. "But they're mostly gone."

Marly bit her bottom lip. "I'll call my mom."

Cate's heart nearly broke for the girl who was clearly nervous about being left behind. "Tell you what. How about we give you a ride home? We have plenty of room in the van."

Her green eyes opened wide. "Oh, no! I don't want to bother you. I can wait for my mother to finish showing the property—"

"You won't be a bother and I'm sure you'd rather be home than standing here waiting. Come on. Let's get going."

Marly looked from the dark window to Cate, then back toward the gym. Finally, she gave a tiny jerky nod. "Okay. If you're sure."

"I'm sure. Let's go."

The parking lot was vacant by the time Cate made her way to the van. There was no way she'd leave Marly behind. True, Alec could have driven the girl home, but because she was ready to go, why leave her behind?

In the van, Cate waited for the seat belt clicks and then pulled out of the now-vacant parking lot. The twins and Lindsay told jokes all the way to Marly's house and Cate encouraged their fun, more so once the teen offered a silly story herself. Laughter felt great. Especially because it was the first time since the fire she'd been able to relax enough to really laugh.

And then she noticed them. The headlights in her rearview mirror. Too close to their rear bumper.

She sped up.

So did the other car.

She turned.

The vehicle behind her did the same.

Cate's heart thudded in her chest and the laughter in the rear of the van shrilled in her head. She had to bite her tongue to keep from asking the kids to quiet down. It would serve no purpose to scare them. It could just be a coincidence.

She found herself thinking of Rand, wishing he were here to see this, so that maybe he'd finally believe that she had nothing to do with the lab, and that someone seemed to be after her. Or maybe she just wished he were with her because he made her feel…safe. The thought caught her off guard for a moment.

She pulled into the gas station. When she gathered

her frayed nerves enough to get out, she topped off the tank, scanning the street for anything suspicious. But what wasn't suspicious in the dark?

"Lord, help me."

Cate climbed back into the van and pulled out of the station. She prayed all the way to Marly's house. When she drove into the driveway, the black compact in the open garage and the light in the front window were the most welcome sights she'd seen in ages.

"Thanks, Miss Cate," Marly said as she jumped out.

"You're welcome. And how about if we make it our routine from now on? I'll bring you home, so you and your mom don't have to worry about it."

Again, Marly's awkwardness struck Cate. "I don't want to bother you," the girl stammered. "I'll be fine."

"But I won't. I'll worry. So do me a favor and let me bring you. For my peace of mind."

The twins and Lindsay piped up.

"Yeah, Marly."

"Come with us."

"You can tell us more stories."

A car sped down the street, but was gone before Cate had a chance to catch a glimpse, much less spot its driver. Icy fingers of fear crawled up her spine. She glanced at the lit house, at the dark street, at the girl just outside the van.

"Okay," Cate said, fighting to keep her voice normal. "Time to go."

She watched Marly go inside and then, with every ounce of strength she could muster, pulled out into the street and drove home.

During the drive, she debated whether or not to call

Rand. On the one hand, he did make her feel safe. On the other, his suspicion infuriated her. By the time she got home, silence had won the battle. She couldn't stomach the thought of having to defend herself. Not that night.

She didn't relax until she'd thrown both deadbolts at home.

FIVE

The next day, as Cate walked into the house after picking up her crew from Lindsay's flute lesson and the boys' drum lessons, the twins nearly tripped her on their rush inside. "Hey! Watch where you're going, and let me check all that homework you say you did while you waited for each other's lesson to finish."

They apologized, then went for their book bags and hurried to change into play clothes. Lindsay went upstairs, her nose in the book du jour. Cate took out an iced tea glass, hit the fridge for the fresh pitcher she'd brewed before heading to school and settled down at the kitchen table to enjoy her favorite drink.

The phone rang.

She groaned, but picked up. "Hello?"

"Miss Caldwell?"

"Uh-huh."

The woman on the other end identified herself as the charge nurse at the ICU. "Just wanted to tell you your dad's been upgraded and we'll be moving him to the regular surgical floor first thing in the morning."

"Really?"

"Really."

A sense of lightness flowed through her and she stumbled back into her chair.

Thank you, Jesus. "Thank you."

"No problem. I figured you'd want some good news to brighten your evening."

"You have no idea."

The nurse laughed, insisted she did and hung up.

Cate sat with the phone receiver clutched tight in her fist, certain she'd crumble and fall if she tried to stand. She hadn't realized how tense she'd been since she'd answered Neal's call about her dad. Maybe Dena had known what she was talking about after all. Maybe Cate had been under more stress than she realized for a lot longer than she'd thought.

The metallic ring of the old-fashioned turnkey doorbell jangled her out of her thoughts. Her heart pounded in her chest and her breath spurted out in shallow, nervous puffs. With every ounce of determination, she rose and pushed away from the table. She had to get a grip. Bad news had made her as tight as a violin string. Now, however, she couldn't let good news turn her into a noodle.

But when she got to the door, nerves threatened to rattle her again. Rand Mason stood on the front porch, as handsome, strong and confident as ever.

She braced herself. "Hi—"

Twin tornadoes sped up the stairs behind her. She winced. "Hey! Keep it down, you guys. I'm trying to talk here."

"Sorry" floated to her, and soon the sounds of the kids chattering overhead told her they'd probably stay out of the way—for a minute or two at least. She turned back to Rand. "What's wrong?"

He dragged his gaze back from the top of the stairs and for a moment, seemed to consider his answer. Then he smiled, but his smile didn't reach his gaze. "Is that a greeting or what? But I guess I deserve it after our lunch. I might have come down on you a bit hard."

"Might have?" She shook her head and offered a conciliatory smile of her own. "Sorry. I realize you have a job to do. It must be a delayed reaction to everything that's happened."

"Gotcha. I can understand how much it's stressed you out." He shrugged. "That's why I'm here. I figured you might want a hand at this point."

"A hand?"

"Sure. With the kids. You have a job, Joe's in ICU—"

"On his way out." She lifted the phone receiver she still held. "I just hung up with the hospital. They're moving him to a regular surgical floor in the morning."

"That's great news. So glad to hear it."

"Anyway, I can handle things from here on in—"

"I'm sure you can, but you don't have to do it all alone. And I hear you've just taken on the teen girls' youth group."

"Someone's been gossiping."

Reed laughed. "Your name was posted on the leadership board at church. I noticed when I went to the men's Bible study last night."

"You're in that study?"

"No…" He shook his head, flattened his lips, shuffled his feet. "No, I'm not."

Her question had made him uncomfortable. She wondered why, but felt she had no right to ask.

When the silence between them grew awkward, he went on. "They wanted me to speak on fire safety issues in the workplace and at home. A couple of the guys are business owners and everyone needs basic knowledge in the house."

"As you can imagine, we have more extinguishers around here than a fireworks factory and Dad thinks a smoke alarm is *the* decorative statement. We're all set."

"That's not why I'm here—"

CRAAAAASH!

Rand lunged for the stairs. "Whoa!"

Cate groaned and did the same.

"Aunt Catey!" Tommy wailed. "Robby kicked the soccer ball into the hall closet mirror."

"Did not, fungus foot. I didn't kick it into the mirror. It sorta…um…rolled away from my foot and into the mirror."

"No way."

"Yes way."

"Nana-nana-naaaah-nah!"

If it weren't for the mess she had to clean up, Cate would have laughed—so long as the boys couldn't see her. But tonight exhaustion threatened to crumple her to the ground.

"That," Rand said, humor in his deep voice, "tells me it's a good thing I came. Don't you think it'll go better if we split the job? You can deal with your Beckham wannabe, and I can take over broom duty."

Rand's offer tempted—oh, how it tempted—and at

that moment, Cate couldn't come up with one single, solitary reason to refuse him.

He gave a nod toward the commotion. "I've missed enough of the kids' lives while I was away. If you'll remember, they're my cousins…second cousins? Once removed? Something like that."

His confusion made her smile. "I do forget, especially because you've been gone for so long. Beats me what the father's cousin is to them—officially speaking, that is."

"So, will you share your dustpan?"

She took the first step up. "Knock yourself out. It's hanging from an organizer behind the kitchen door. The broom's right there, too."

Rand saluted her, then strode down the hall. Cate continued up the stairs, enveloped in a sense of the surreal. She'd always resented Rand in high school—he'd been Mr. Perfect. And at lunch the other day, he'd flat-out told her he suspected her participation in a meth lab and a fire. And yet, tonight he'd shown up…to help her? And she hadn't shut the door on him?

Did he ever throw her off-kilter…

And not just because of his suspicion. This Rand, the one who understood what she was going through, who'd come to her aid, had her reacting in ways she never would have thought possible. This Rand was too attractive for her own good, too dangerous.

She feared she was falling under his spell, well-recognized back when they were both in high school. All the girls had been gaga over him. Cate imagined grown women were, too.

She sighed. She *wanted* to give him a chance. Most

men ran away from women with kids. What sane woman would send away a great-looking guy who'd just acknowledged he'd been tough on her and who wanted to shoulder some of the care for her trio of munchkins?

Even if the man in question was her once-upon-a-time nemesis, Cate wouldn't turn him away. Heaven help her, she was too curious about him.

If he hit her again with his suspicions, she'd show him the door. Until then, she'd enjoy the company of someone willing to help, someone who smiled in the face of the havoc created by her three charges. Someone with beautiful blue eyes.

As Rand sat at the Caldwell's kitchen table after a bedtime snack with Cate and the kids, he had to admit that the children seemed healthy, well-adjusted, happy, and while quirky and rambunctious, well cared-for and much loved. He could hear Cate upstairs talking to them, trying to get them settled into bed.

Cate struck him as a puzzle. There was no denying the appealing woman she seemed to have become, with her rich, wavy brown hair and big, dark eyes. Her easy laughter tickled a dark corner of his heart and she hadn't skimped on the humor, even while dealing with the hallway mess. She'd teased the twins and Lindsay, reinforced her rules and done it all in a way the kids had received well and even accepted. Lindsay and the twins loved her, just as she clearly loved them. Anyone could see it in their interactions. But could he trust Cate?

Still her disturbing presence at the scene of the fire, and the photos. As of a few hours ago, more evidence pointed to her. How did she fit into that picture?

As soon as he had the opportunity to break the news to her, he'd probably find out.

He'd asked Ethan and Hal to let him tell her about the body at the theater. He wanted to see her face, her expression, gauge her reaction when he told her.

So here he was. In Cate's kitchen. Waiting for her to listen to bedtime prayers—how weird was that? Cate Caldwell, praying. The bedtime prayer routine made him uncomfortable. Rand didn't get the God thing. If there really was an all-powerful Almighty God, why did He let such hideous things happen in the world He'd created?

Cup in hand, Rand left the kitchen and wandered through the downstairs rooms. The Caldwell home, a lovely, stately, older place, had wonderful moldings and rich hardwood floors, and the living room boasted an old fireplace with original tile and a classic mantel.

Rand could almost see Joe in the big leather armchair, his feet up on the matching ottoman, jazz on the stereo, a biography in his hands. In fact, one of those biographies was still sitting on the small side table next to a stack of photos.

Rand's curiosity got the better of him. But the minute he fanned through the pictures, he froze. An image of Cate and Sam Burns greeted his gaze. And there was a letter with the photos.

He started to read.

Sam had written about her waiting for him, how they belonged together, how they'd be reunited soon now that he'd done his time. That didn't sound like they'd had no contact, as Cate had said.

How was she going to refute this?

Unreasonable though it might be, Rand felt betrayed. He wanted Cate to be as innocent as she said she was.

This had never happened to him before—he'd never cared personally for anyone involved in one of his investigations. It threw him off, big time.

The depth of Rand's disappointment surprised him as much as the strength of his earlier need to know who Cate was now. Why had it mattered so much? Had it just been for the sake of the investigation? Or had it been for the sake of his cousin's kids?

He sighed. His need to know probably had everything to do with the pretty woman who'd come out to the fire. The daughter who'd worried about her hero father. The aunt so devoted to three orphaned youngsters.

That woman touched a part of him Rand would rather keep out of reach.

He checked his watch. She was taking a long time with those prayers.

When Cate came downstairs ten minutes later, he followed her into the kitchen, gave her the time to pour a glass of iced tea and then sat across from her. She took a long drink, placed the glass on the table, laced her fingers and finally met his gaze.

"Thanks for your help tonight, Rand."

"I have to confess, Cate. The kids weren't the only reason I came by tonight. I've got questions for you. And information to share."

She jerked as though he'd stabbed her with a pin.

He continued. "We have a positive ID on the corpse. Do you want to revisit your answer about how long it's been since you last had contact with Sam Burns?"

At first, she frowned. Then comprehension dawned.

She shook her head, her gaze fixed on Rand. "Are you telling me Sam…died in the fire?"

He nodded. "Dental records match. It seems Sam didn't waste much time after his release before going right back to his old tricks."

Unless she was an accomplished actress, his news came as a surprise, which he hadn't expected. Not after the letter he'd just found.

"So when was the last time you talked to Sam?"

Her eyes flashed. "I told you already. The last time I had any contact with him was right before the accident."

So she was sticking to her story. Fine. He'd try another tack. He pulled Sam's letter from his pocket and held it up.

SIX

As he waited for Cate to answer, the color drained from her face. Her hand darted out and clenched his wrist.

"Look!"

Her hoarse croak made him turn, but he saw nothing. Rand turned back. Her big brown eyes still stared over his shoulder, her features drawn and pale, her breathing a series of quick, shallow sips.

"What? What are you looking at?"

Her fingers dug deeper into his skin. Her other hand rose and the finger with which she pointed out the window shook. Again, Rand looked where Cate indicated, seeing nothing of note. But he couldn't accuse her of pretending. Her fear was so great it radiated off her in waves.

"A man..." Cate's voice shook. "The window."

He shot her another look, then turned. "Are you sure? I can't see anything."

She shook herself. "Not...not anymore. But he *was* there. I saw him, for just a flash of a second."

Rand stood and walked to the sink. He leaned over the spotless stainless rectangle and stared out. By the light of the moon, he only saw the shadowed shapes of shrubs and the double garage at the end of the drive.

He faced Cate again. "There's nothing there. Are you sure—"

"Of course, I'm sure!" She pushed away from the table and marched over to him, glaring. "I'm not crazy nor am I a nutty character in some movie about ghosts. There was a man staring in the window. I know what I saw. Just like that car that followed us home from church."

Rand blinked and shook his head. "Car? Followed you? Why didn't you report it?"

She blushed. "I hoped I was imagining things. Just being paranoid after the attack at the theater. But now I know I saw what I saw. A car followed us to Marly Wooten's house after youth group—she's one of the girls in my group. And I saw a man stare in that window not five minutes ago. Someone is after me."

Rand didn't know what to believe. She could be a fabulous, Oscar-worthy actress. On the other hand, someone could be following her. She might have seen something that threatened someone.

"Only one way to know for sure." He headed for the back door. "Do you have a light out back?"

Her jaw tight, a fine line across her forehead, she nodded, went to the switch plate near the hallway arch and flicked up the bottom toggle. Through the window and the glass half of the back door, a golden glow penetrated the dark.

"Let's go check it out."

Rand gave a thorough scrutiny to the flower bed beneath the kitchen window. To his shock, the shrub's branches were twisted out of shape and a partial print of a running shoe could be seen in the rich, dark earth.

He shot Cate a look. Fear tightened her features. He reached in his pocket and dialed 9-1-1.

She shuddered. "It feels rotten to be right."

An hour later, after Hal, Ethan and Rand had gone over the backyard with halogen lamps and evidence-gathering crews, the two law enforcement officers went their way, and Rand walked Cate to the front door.

It was time to go—past time, really—but he found himself unable to leave. He turned to say goodbye, and the fine line between her brows sparked a twinge of concern.

"Are you going to be okay?" he asked.

She shrugged. "Of course. I have to be. Dad and the kids need me."

She struck him as fragile, likely to tip over at the lightest breeze. But he knew there was more strength to her than that. Still, the stress had done a number on her.

As he stared, she seemed to draw on inner reserves. She stood straighter and pasted on a weak smile. "I'll be fine. And thanks for your help. With the kids, sure, but especially with…"

Her voice died off as she waved toward the back of the house.

Her gratitude left him wanting to do more. Starting with wrapping his arms around her. The urge was so strong, he couldn't fight it off, so he went with it.

"Oh!" she said on a breathy gasp.

He should have released her, but she felt so good in his arms. And he knew no one was going to hurt her while she stood there at his side. As the warmth of her breath brushed his neck, he knew it was time to go— for real, this time.

He stepped back, his arms awkward at his sides. "Well…ah…it just seemed like you needed a hug."

Her eyes, already wide and staring, opened a fraction more. Great. He really had to leave before he made a fool of himself.

"Okay!" His voice sounded too cheerful, even to him. *Beat it, Mason. Now!* "So…I'll see you. And let me know if anything else scares you…happens. You know."

Irritated at his clumsiness, he spun and jogged down the front steps and to his car at the curb.

"Fool, fool, fool!" He should have focused on the intruder. He'd had a professional reason to linger. But then he'd gone and wrapped his arms around her. What good was that going to be for their investigation?

Someone had been in Cate's backyard, but whoever it was hadn't left much evidence behind. True, they'd found a partial print from a man's size-ten running shoe, but matching it would present a challenge.

Hal, Ethan and Rand had questioned Cate again and she'd told them about the car following her home. While her answers had seemed to come easily enough, she'd kept her emotions and expressions under tight control after her initial shock. Rand hadn't been able to get a good read off her and he doubted Hal or Ethan had done much better either.

The question now was whether Cate was involved with the meth dealer or whether she presented a threat to him. So far, questions continued to pile up. A discouraging lack of answers plagued their investigation.

While they did have a witness to the original fire, they weren't too sure what that witness had really seen. One of the high school senior girls who'd gone to see the film had stayed behind, waiting for her ride. She'd given them a vague description of a man she'd seen. But any number of men might have been in the vicinity of the theater for legitimate reasons that night.

They couldn't discount the possibility she was trying to cover her true reason for lingering later than she should have by concocting a story about a man near the theater's back door.

The lack of answers was driving Rand crazy, especially because he'd failed to extract any from Cate. Because of that he didn't feel he had a better handle on her.

He hadn't eased his mind about the kids either.

He had, however, against his better judgment, noted the sparkle in her dark brown eyes and the light sprinkle of cinnamon freckles on her straight nose. He'd especially noticed, and appreciated, her quick smile throughout the earlier evening, when they'd spent time with the kids.

She had a self-deprecating sense of humor and yet there was plenty of strength behind the easy smiles and the obvious determination to care for the kids.

The ease he'd felt with her before he discovered the letter unnerved him. He'd felt comfortable at the Caldwell home. More than that, he'd felt right with Cate. He'd had an odd sense of belonging, of common purpose, and he'd told himself, more than once, it stemmed from their love for the kids.

But Cate Caldwell held an inexplicable appeal for

him. When they were in the same room, he couldn't keep his gaze from straying to her, no matter what the subject of the visit or discussion might be.

Not good.

What if…?

No! It wouldn't do any good to go down the speculation route. No matter how Cate struck him, she was in one way or another involved in his current investigation.

She impressed him, he realized. She seemed to accept full responsibility for her choices and for the consequences they'd had. That appealed to his sense of right and wrong. Could she be involved in the drug trade and still speak as she did about the accident?

If he wanted answers he'd have to stay close, keep an eye on her, build a relationship of some sort.

To Rand's dismay, the prospect held powerful appeal.

When she closed the front door behind Rand, Cate allowed herself a deep, relieved sigh. She understood why he'd felt the need to question her as extensively as he had, but the experience had been arduous. Understanding didn't make it feel any better.

She much preferred to think about how he'd helped her tuck the kids into bed. Their gazes had met over Lindsay's bed and she knew a special bond existed between them. It came from shared loss and love for three innocents, but she and Rand would always share that special something.

And that made his suspicion hard to take. How could he see her with the kids and continue to think she'd have anything to do with drugs?

If anything, his suspicion made her determined to

prove herself to him. She wanted him to see how much she'd changed since that fateful day. She wanted to clear her name…because she wanted to get to know him better.

At times, the sharp stare from those blue eyes took her back to the days after the accident. Fast-forward eight years and here he was again. It still amazed Cate how far the tentacles of a bad choice could reach.

A stupid old album full of childish pictures. A criminal's obsessive thoughts behind bars. An incriminating letter.

Didn't Rand understand that just the thought of Sam literally turned her stomach? How could he think she'd want anything to do with the person whose substance abuse had taken her sister's life?

Even after every one of her denials, her father's number-two man had continued to press her. She could see why he'd been, and still was, such a successful investigator. He had the instincts of a pit bull.

In the end, the best she came up with was to repeat the only thing she could say for sure. "I don't know what made me so self-destructive for a while back then. I just know it's not anything I'm proud of, and Sam's not anyone I'd have anything to do with these days."

Whether it satisfied him or not, laying it all out was as honest as she could get. Cate really didn't know why she'd taken a turn down the path of self-destruction as a teen. It had been a stupid thing to do. To live each day under that burden was tough. By the many mercies of her Savior, she managed. But only by His mercy and through His grace.

These days, she lived her life as close to the Lord

as she could, clinging to His Word, claiming His promises, rejoicing in His steadfast forgiveness. Beyond that, all she had was trust. Cate trusted very little in life. She trusted her father, who'd loved her even in the middle of immeasurable grief at the loss of his oldest daughter and son-in-law. She also trusted the faith she held dear to her heart.

She had nothing else, not really. Not when it came to this, the defining issue of her life. And she considered herself rich, indeed, incredibly blessed to have that assurance, that certainty in God's love and compassion. He was faithful and on her side. She knew that for sure.

The Lord had promised He would never leave her nor forsake her. She could trust in Him.

Rand? She'd have to get to know him better before she could ever trust him. Especially because he made no secret of his doubts. Exhausted, she made her way up the stairs to her room.

At nine-thirty on Saturday morning, the house spun madly in its usual three-ring-circus way. After a breakfast of pancakes and sausage, Cate had sent the kids off to take care of their chores while she put the finishing touches on the trademark cinnamon rolls she'd promised Alec. But every few seconds, or so it seemed, a new ruckus broke out, requiring her intervention.

She knew for a fact the mixing of cream cheese, powdered sugar, vanilla and milk did not make for a time-intensive endeavor. Amazing how in her case making frosting had morphed into a nearly hour-long project.

"Aunt Catey…!"

Yup. Yet another interruption. Lindsay's wail drew a groan from the depths of Cate's frustrated pastry chef's heart.

"Ignore them, my girl, and get back to that pile of clean towels I gave you. Fold them into thirds—"

"It's not about the towels," her niece said from the kitchen doorway.

"What's it—"

One glance told Cate what it had all been about. Fat, white, shaving-cream caterpillars draped Lindsay from head to toe. Beneath the mess, the little girl's downtrodden expression stung Cate's heart. It triggered a memory, a remembrance just out of her reach, but she couldn't put a finger on the exact image.

That's when Alec walked in the back door, as she'd asked him to do. He froze at the sight of the foamy Lindsay, his gaze zipping between aunt and niece.

"Hmm…looks like you might need a hand with the boys."

She squared her shoulders and shook her head. "Nothing a good threat to nix this afternoon's Major League Soccer game on cable won't cure."

"Aunt Catey…"

"How about you give me a hand with those baked goods you like so much, Alec? If you'll spread the rolls with the frosting, I can run up and deal with my two rats."

"Only if I get to lick the spoon and bowl when I'm done."

"You got yourself a deal."

The boys apologized to Lindsay when Cate threatened their game-viewing pleasure. "I'm sure you'll do a good job helping Lindsay clean up the shaving cream and then pitch in to put away the linens."

Twin sighs were a study in long-suffering, but they agreed to do the right thing. Cate headed back downstairs to her culinary concoction. Back in the kitchen, Alec scraped a blob of frosting off the wooden spoon and popped it in his mouth.

"Delicious!" He pointed upward with the spoon. "All squared away?"

She nodded, took two large mugs from the cabinet above the coffeemaker and then filled them to the rim. "For right now. Never a dull moment and all that." She plunked the mugs on the table. "Enjoy."

Alec demolished a huge roll in seconds. "Tell me. Did I overburden you when I asked you to help out at church? You're wearing a lot of hats these days."

Different answers warred in Cate, but it took her less than a second to respond. "Not really. My work at the day care is more supervisory than hands-on. I have an excellent staff and I have to learn to delegate. These three are a full-time proposition, but they're no worse than any other single mom's kids."

"I'll be honest—and a bit selfish. I think you're going to be phenomenal with the girls. Plus I need the help while Beth deals with this crazy pregnancy and all our babies."

His frazzled father-to-be look made Cate smile. "You've got my help. So don't worry, okay?"

Forty-five minutes later, Alec tapped a pen against the legal pad they'd used for their Tuckerpalooza lists and then grabbed another roll. "Looking good."

As he munched, a question that had tickled Cate's

conscience refused to be silenced any longer. "I wanted to run something by you, something that really matters to me, and is part of why I agreed to help with the youth group. Don't you think, after all that's happened in town, we should start a drug awareness and prevention program at church?"

Alec frowned. "That might be overkill. Our program at the high school runs year-round and is very explicit. We don't want to bombard the kids and desensitize them. If that happens, we'll blow any chance we might have to do any good."

Cate's initial reaction was to object. But the man was an expert in the field. "I just don't want to lose any more teens—"

The doorbell rang. She hadn't expected anyone and Saturday mornings rarely brought unexpected visitors. "I'll be right back."

Alec stood and followed her toward the front of the house. "Oh, I should get going. I've taken up a lot of your time and I'm sure you have plans for the rest of the day."

As she opened the door, two sets of feet pounded down the stairs. A third set padded softly in their wake.

"Who's here?"

"Can we take a break?"

"Aunt Catey…?"

Rand stood on her front porch. In spite of his sweat-stained hoodie, running shorts and shoes, he looked like he belonged on the pages of a men's magazine.

"Hi. What a surprise. I didn't expect to see you today."

She felt Rand's laser-like blue gaze take in the scene. As it had before, his perusal made her feel as though she disappointed him. Well, maybe that was a bit too strong. Maybe she just felt discomfort at his slight distaste.

Then their gazes met, and Cate felt a jolt of energy. She'd never experienced anything like it before and didn't particularly welcome it. Not when Rand made no secret he questioned her honesty.

Yet there it was. She couldn't deny it. She was more attracted to Rand Mason than she'd ever been to any other man. And he was standing on her front porch, for some as-yet-unvoiced reason.

That's when she noticed the tension in the air. The two men stood, feet wide, Rand with arms crossed, Alec with hands in his pants pockets, measuring each other. Good grief! They might as well have been a pair of German shepherds in a short and narrow dog run.

The kids stared in fascination.

She nearly groaned out loud. "Alec misses home cooking while his wife's in the hospital waiting for their triplets' births. I took pity on his need for baked goods."

The men exchanged a wary greeting. Then an awkward silence.

Alec blinked first. "Well. Like I said, I have to get going. Thanks for the cinnamon rolls. And I'll see you at church tomorrow."

Cate wrapped her arms around her middle as Alec strode down the front steps and across the yard toward his home. Behind her, the kids' curiosity practically bristled. Before her, Rand's attitude rankled.

She took a deep breath. "Can I help you?"

He shook his head and smiled—a smile that didn't do a thing to warm those icy blue eyes. "The Rotary

Club is sponsoring a hayride and bonfire. I thought the kids might enjoy going."

Alone? It took every ounce of Cate's strength to keep from blurting out her question. "We've already planned to watch an MLS game on cable this afternoon."

Rand gave a brief nod. "The hayride's not until seven. The game won't go on that long, will it?"

"YES!" Robby yelled. "I mean, no. The game starts at three. It'll be finished by then. Please, Aunt Catey. Please, can we go?"

"Please, please, *pleeeeeeeze!*" Tommy echoed.

In the face of such enthusiasm, she'd have felt like an ogre if she refused. "Looks like we're on, Captain Mason. I guess we'll be roasting marshmallows tonight."

He grinned and the kids cheered. As he jogged back toward the sidewalk, Cate couldn't help but wonder if she'd just agreed to a date with Rand Mason.

SEVEN

Rand arrived at the Caldwell home at six-fifteen, as he and Cate had agreed. The doorbell's ring sparked a chorus of excited yells and cheers. He smiled.

He needed to strengthen his relationship with the kids. He hadn't done much in that regard during the years he'd been away and he acknowledged that personal failure. But now he had a chance to remedy that.

And more.

A number of reasons drew him to the Caldwell family. His friendship with Joe and his cousin's kids were only two of them.

The door opened and a thick patchwork quilt came at him. "Hi, Rand. I checked the weather forecast," Cate said. "A cold front's coming in tonight. The wind's expected to kick up, too, so this should keep the kids warm in the hay wagon."

Rand stared at the pretty woman who'd shoved the pink and purple fabric at him. Her cheeks glowed with a rosy tint and her brown eyes sparkled with a rich warmth that drew him closer. At that moment, he surrendered. He'd been looking forward to the time they'd planned to spend together, kids or no kids. And his anticipation had nothing to do with the pending investigation. Every day that went by, Cate Caldwell intrigued him more.

He gave her a wry smile. "You don't happen to have a more…um…masculine blanket we can use, do you?"

Cate studied the offending fabric and then ran a slow look from his head to his toes. To his surprise, her perusal made him uncomfortable. And the fussy feminine blanket had nothing to do with his dropping comfort level.

What did she see when she took his measure?

When she grinned and her eyes twinkled, he realized he'd set himself up. "You're not afraid of your more feminine side, now, are you?" She tucked her tongue firmly in her cheek. "A great, big fireman like you?"

"Aw…Aunt Catey!" Tommy, bundled in a plaid flannel jacket, mittens and cap peered around Cate and stared at Rand. "I'm not sitting under that sissy thing of yours. The other guys on the team'll all make fun of me."

Rand couldn't corral the grin that tipped the right side of his mouth. "From the mouths of babes. And just so you know where I stand, I wouldn't do a thing to take away from your feminine appeal. You look great."

The mulberry wool coat and the cream-colored knit hat that tamed her tawny waves enhanced Cate's coloring. The pink comforter provided the perfect frame. Rand felt the urge to run a finger down one silky-looking, flushed cheek, but common sense held him back.

As did her widened eyes and stunned expression. He'd thrown her off balance with his compliment. He hadn't meant to, but at least he wasn't the only one feeling the strange pull between them. And fortunately, she didn't seem offended or upset by his words.

Cate herded her three charges out of the house and locked the front door. "Come on, guys. I just grabbed the quilt on my bed. It was the first thing I got my hands on."

With a sheepish grin, he stepped aside as Cate headed down the front steps. "Let's give your aunt a break, guys. Real men can do pink and purple any time."

Cate laughed. "I'm so glad you approve, Captain Mason." She turned to the twins. "Now, Tommy, you get the way-back seat, and Robby. the middle-back one. Lindsay, you ride next to Robby."

The two boys grumbled on their way to the van, their shoulders crashing accidentally on purpose two or three times. Lindsay tiptoed after them.

Rand tucked the blanket under his arm. "Is there room for me, too, Aunt Catey?"

Her blush made her look young, vulnerable and innocent. The effect took him by surprise. Had she really escaped the hardening that came with the choices she'd made as a teen? True, she was older now, but not that much older, maybe all of twenty-five.

She smiled. "Hey, you've just scored the shotgun seat, Rand. That's big around here. Really big."

Rand threw his head back and laughed. "Hayride and marshmallows, here we come."

"Woo-hoo!" Tommy crowed as they piled out of the van at the hayride field. "There's Phil Britton. Can I go say hi, Aunt Catey? Huh? Huh? Can I?"

"Me, too," Robby begged. "He's awesome."

Cate spotted the captain of the high school varsity soccer team surrounded by a group of teens. The popular athlete had earned his referee's license and he officiated the boys' games, to their enormous thrill. Phil was said to have a brilliant future, with college scholarships and a possible professional career included.

"We can spare a few minutes."

Tommy and Robby ran over and high-fived Phil, and Cate, who'd had him babysit a couple of times, gave him a hug. "Great game last night," she said. "You had a nice hat trick."

Two other boys, also on the varsity team, whistled.

"Star power!" one cried in a teasing voice.

Another one pumped a fist. "Duuuuude! Three goals."

Four girls giggled, sending the whole group into a riff of adolescent giddiness.

Cate glanced at the crowd waiting for the next wagon. She recognized just about everyone there, a bonus that came from living in the same small town where she'd grown up.

"Cate!" a woman called.

She turned and spotted Abby Colby, the high school foods and nutrition teacher. She stepped away from the chatty teens and closer to her friend. "Are you and J.J. here with the team?"

Abby's jet-black ponytail flew from side to side as she shook her head. "Not officially. This is our date night for the week. Can you believe *the coach* himself took time away from his soccer team to spend the evening with his wife during playoff season?"

Cate laughed. "He's crazy about you and you know it."

"Yeah, but the team made playoffs and I know that, too."

"Is she complaining again?" Zoe sauntered up, a wink and a grin taking the sting away from her words. "I wouldn't mind a guy with J.J.'s focus and ability to care for kids. Where do they mint them?"

Cate swatted Zoe on the shoulder. "Who let you out of the hospital, you vampire you? Aren't there sick people who need blood drawn tonight?"

"I'm due back in an hour and a half."

After catching up, Abby walked away to join her husband and Zoe headed toward her car. Cate made her way back to where the twins and Lindsay still stood in awe of the star athletes. Rand approached Cate.

"Looks like they'll make a bundle for the new library," Rand said, looking at the long lines.

"You know what life is like around here. Logantonians usually support all the civic fund-raising efforts."

The rumble of wagon wheels alerted them to the arrival of the next wagon. The tractor driver dropped off his current load of customers, then waved the next passengers onto the hay.

Cate helped Lindsay up on one bale, had the twins sit between their sister and their soccer hero and then watched Rand sit down at her nephews' feet. She tucked the quilt around Lindsay's legs, before joining Rand right in front of the little girl.

"If you get cold," she told the twins, "there's plenty of blanket here."

Robby and Tommy scowled at the comforter as they scooted closer to the teens. Rand grinned at Cate.

Moments later, the driver cranked up the tractor's

engine and the farm vehicle tugged the heavy-laden wagon out to the fields and toward the bonfire, whose red glow burnished the dark, fall sky with fingers of deep gold.

The spicy scent of fall blended with the chill in the air. Cate had always loved the waning season for its colors and rich anticipation. A hayride was the quintessential event leading up to Thanksgiving. As the tractor chugged along, the wagon wheels dipped and rose over ruts in the field. She rocked against the hay bales at her back. Every so often, she found herself bouncing off Rand's solid shoulder. He didn't seem to mind.

The next time she bumped into him, he chuckled and wrapped an arm around her shoulders to steady her.

Cate found herself staring at his blue eyes, which didn't seem particularly cold just then. The arm holding her felt right, as though it belonged where it lay.

"Having fun?" His voice rang low, a bit huskier than usual.

She couldn't have played coy even if she'd wanted to. "I love this!"

His grin broadened as he released her. "I used to come with Mom and Dad every year. We'd do the marshmallows and stuff and then go home, where Mom had left apple cider in the crockery cooker. That spicy, hot mug was the best drink ever, especially when we sat in front of the fire."

"I don't remember seeing you here and we used to come every year, too."

"You were probably too busy being a girl. I remember the giggly cliques every fall." He gave a theatrical shiver. "They scared all the guys."

She gave him a teasing punch on the shoulder. "I don't think anything's ever scared you."

"You'd be surprised." His smile vanished as his expression grew serious. "Running into a burning building, certain someone's life depends on you, is a sobering experience. Firefighters are scared. We just learn to live with that fear."

His intensity invited respect. And admiration. "I could never do what you do."

It dawned on Cate they might as well have been the only people on the wagon. Rand fascinated her. She was enjoying herself far more than she'd expected. But as the ride progressed, her enjoyment dimmed. Over the cheerful ruckus, she heard the behavior of the jocks, Phil included, deteriorate.

Eventually, their language grew crude. Others burst into nervous laughter when one blurted out an expletive.

"Whoa, guys!" Cate said angrily.

Robby's eyes grew saucer-sized. Tommy dropped his chin onto his chest, clearly embarrassed. Lindsay, even in the evening darkness, looked chalk-white with shock.

Rand turned to the jock. "Hey, man! Watch that kind of stuff. There are little kids here, okay?"

Out of the corner of her eye, Cate caught Phil's embarrassed look. She turned to Rand. "Thanks."

He winked. "Just protecting the citizens from fire, ma'am. Flames come in different varieties, you know."

The respite didn't last. Off-color jokes started up again and one of the more outrageous boys draped an arm around one of the girls and nuzzled her neck.

"Hey!" Cate objected. "Not here."

"What are ya?" the would-be Romeo grumbled. "The Love Buster or something?"

The other soccer players found his comment hilarious. Romeo, however, did move a fraction of an inch away from the girl while humming the theme song to the movie *Ghostbusters.* The teens did clean up their language and public displays of affection, but their excessive silliness continued for the rest of the ride.

When the tractor stopped, Rand echoed Cate's need to get away. He hopped right down, then turned to help the twins. Cate reached for Lindsay, setting the little girl down at her side.

"Hey, Aunt Cate," Lindsay said. "I've gotta go right now!"

At her side, Rand chuckled. "Go ahead. I'll stay with the boys."

Cate hurried her niece to the portable toilets the Rotary Club had set up, and stood outside to wait for the girl to finish. Too bad their evening had been marred by the soccer players' crudeness—

Without any warning, a large mass hurtled into Cate's back. She lost her footing, stumbled, flailed to regain her balance, but couldn't, and ultimately flew forward.

As she fell, she heard a harsh whisper. "Mind your own business! Stay out of it!"

She dropped toward the hay-covered ground. "Hey! Who's there?"

No one answered, and by the time Lindsay came out of the toilet, Cate was back on her feet. Half of her burned with irritation, the other half shook with fear. The memory of the person who'd attacked her outside the theater loomed ominous in her thoughts.

She led her niece back toward the bonfire. As she approached, Rand stepped up to her. His brilliant blue eyes burned into hers, and concern showed across his face. "Are you okay? What happened?"

She blinked, tried to sort out her thoughts, but before she could do so, he reached out and placed his hands on her shoulders. The gentle contact made her feel secure, cared for, treasured somehow.

"Um…I think so, but someone ran right into me." For a moment, she debated whether to tell him about the whisper, but then decided he could make up his mind about it himself. "Whoever hit me did it on purpose, just like the other time. At the theater. Only difference is that this time, he told me to mind my own business."

"Twice, huh? Strange."

Rand's mild words came with a skeptical look, which took care of the rightness she'd been feeling in his arms. She shoved against his rock-solid chest. He got the message, eased his hold on her and slowly, gently set her back on her feet. Cate hated the sense of loss she felt when he let her go. His doubts colored everything between them. And for that reason, she couldn't afford to let him have such an impact on her. She couldn't afford to need him at all.

She retrieved her blanket from where it had fallen on the ground. "Strange or not, he said it. I heard it. But I don't know what he was talking about. Maybe it was one of the kids. They weren't too happy with me when I complained about their behavior."

"You have a point. Maybe that's what it was."

While hers was the most logical decision, Rand didn't

sound convinced. Cate wasn't going to dwell on what had happened, much less on what he thought about it.

Blanket in hand, Cate walked over to the twins and Lindsay. She told the boys to stay within sight at all times and then led her niece to a table where she could prepare a treat to roast.

Once she'd settled Lindsay, she looked for a place to sit. A lone bale remained vacant a few feet behind the circle of marshmallow-roasting attendees closest to the bonfire. Rand joined Cate moments later. "Sorry about that. I wouldn't have brought you and the kids if I'd thought anything like this might happen."

"It's not your fault." She looked around, but didn't see the rowdy teenagers. "Those guys are old enough to know better."

Rand shrugged. "You never can tell."

Despite his neutral response, Cate noticed how intently he scanned the area around the bonfire. Those blue eyes, pale and focused, seemed to pierce even the thickest of shadows at the edge of a nearby clump of trees.

Earlier, it had seemed as though Rand had shelved his suspicions for tonight. Maybe she had made progress with him in the matter of her innocence. She certainly hoped she had.

And maybe her past made her especially sensitive when it came to Rand. Maybe she imagined the worst possible options around him.

She stole another glance at the fire captain. Tall and handsome, he projected a striking presence, and radiated an air of strength with his wide shoulders and broad chest. His legs carried him with long, smooth strides, his assurance obvious. Dark hair, blue-blue eyes, a nose with a bump that spoke of a long-ago fracture and high cheekbones above lean cheeks gave his face an intense expression.

As a woman, she couldn't deny his masculine appeal.

Out of the corner of her eye, she noticed the faint line between his brows. Rand's mind never seemed to quit. She took it as an excuse to ask about the investigation. "Are you ready to tell me who the witness is? How about the plastic thing I found?"

"I did want to talk to you about that, but I figured we'd get a chance later, in private."

A lead balloon would have felt no heavier than the dread that dropped into her middle. A private talk. That sounded ominous. Especially when she considered who wanted to do the talking.

She sighed. Later wasn't going to work. She'd never survive the wait. "I'd rather know now."

Rand looked around, but even Cate could tell everyone was more interested in the bonfire and marshmallows than anything the two of them might discuss. One of his broad shoulders rose and fell. "Look, you know I can't tell you anything about the witness—"

"You know what? I think you've figured out that witness saw nothing. At least, nothing concrete that figures in with the fire. Am I right?"

He looked away.

She crowed. "I knew it! You just thought I'd crack if you made me think someone had seen something that might incriminate me."

She expected him to argue with her, but instead, his next words surprised her. "That thing you found on the sidewalk?"

Cate caught her breath. "Yeah? What was it?"

"The lab says it's an ID badge of some kind."

"Can they identify the owner?"

He shook his head. "It was too damaged for them to lift a name, bar code or any part of the photo. But the lab's not done with it yet. They want to do more, study it with more sensitive equipment, to see if they can get something—anything—from it."

"So it is important."

"Possibly." Cate went to object, but he gave her a tight smile before going on. "Okay. It might be important, but that leaves us with hundreds of people who potentially could have lost the ID. Just think how many jobs require that kind of card."

Her breath came out in a gust of relief. "Mine doesn't."

He crossed his arms as his gaze raked her face. "But you do have a driver's license, don't you? How about a shopping warehouse card? Library card? They're all made from the same kind of material with minor differences."

"Great. That just makes the pool of candidates infinite and finding the owner that much harder."

"Maybe. Maybe not." He arched a brow.

"Rand, I've already told you. I was at home Saturday night. Neal saw me arrive. I wasn't in the theater at all. Besides, if I'd dropped my own card at the scene, do you really think I'd call and hand it to you?"

"Maybe you saw it as the perfect wild goose chase to send us on."

"If suspecting me is the best you can do to investigate the fire, then Loganton's in trouble. We'll never learn who's behind the meth if you keep accusing me.

I know I can do better myself if I snoop around with nothing but curiosity to rely on."

That caught his attention. "That's a terrible idea."

"No worse an idea than me involved with a lab. Or meth." She leaned toward him, intent on persuading him, willing him to see her sincerity. "You have to believe me. I never spoke to Sam after the accident. Never said a word to him during the trial. I lost my sister, you know. The thought of what I'd done turned my stomach. It still affects me to this day."

"So you've said. A number of times."

She let out a loud, frustrated breath. "But I suppose you can't prove something I say I didn't do." When he didn't answer, she added, "The old album in the theater, and the photos and letter Sam sent me don't help matters any, do they?"

"The only fingerprints on those things are yours and Sam's. Plus he sent you a love letter, not just some random note."

Nausea struck. "Don't blame me for Sam's obsession. And as far as fingerprints go, I don't see why there would be any others. It was my album. He must have kept it somewhere while he was in jail, and then retrieved it when he got out."

"Any idea how he wound up with the album in the first place?"

"Beats me. For all I know, he stole it from me and I never noticed. I certainly haven't had any desire to look at photos from that time in my life since the accident."

Rand met her gaze and in the dark, she saw something she hadn't noticed before. The pain of loss still ate at him, too.

He sighed. "That I do believe."

Movement behind Rand at the base of the trees, caught her attention. Unless she was mistaken, someone was sick, vomiting. Two other figures approached the first, one staggering, evidently just as impaired.

Then the first collapsed. Cate leaped to her feet. In that moment, everything clicked. "Don't you move a muscle until I get back. And keep your sister with you," she called out to the twins.

She grabbed Rand's hand and they ran toward the soccer players. As they hurried over, a second boy stumbled, doubled over in pain, clutching his middle. The third—Phil Britton—leaned against a tree and moaned in similar misery. Only feet away, Cate realized the one who'd fallen wasn't moving. His chest was motionless.

"Call 9-1-1," Rand said. "Ask for ambulances. Tell them we have three underage intoxications—looks pretty bad. We might even be looking at possible overdoses."

Their sudden rush from the bonfire had caught the attention of their fellow marshmallow-toasters, making them the object of stares and whispers. As Cate dialed, Alec appeared.

"What's wrong?" he asked, out of breath.

She pointed toward the boys, where Rand was now checking on the one who'd collapsed. As she and Alec watched, another one dropped to his knees. Like a boneless mass, he melted onto the blanket of dead leaves on the ground.

Alec took off to help. "Oh, man…"

The emergency services dispatcher answered. Cate described the situation. "I've got help on the way, miss," the woman finally said. "Just hang on."

Cate prayed on her way back to the bonfire and her kids. Coach Colby ran over to her.

"What's going on?"

"J.J., your players are…sick—in bad shape. Over there."

With a glance that took in everything, J.J.'s jaw turned to steel. He let out a guttural growl.

Cate placed a hand on his arm. "I'm sorry."

"This takes them off the team permanently. School rules. We had our suspicions. Now, though, we know for sure. They can forget scholarships and those spots on college team rosters." He ran to help Rand and Alec.

Cate began to pray again. She prayed for the boys, for Rand and Alec and J.J. She prayed for Loganton and all the kids who could fall prey to a dealer's wares.

Steps away from the twins and Lindsay, she noticed a cluster of kids. A pale, frightened face in the middle of the group practically reached out and grabbed her sympathy. Marly needed comfort, and while Robby, Tommy and Lindsay had been alone for a while, she could see them from where she stood and they were fine.

Marly wasn't.

She reached the teen and wrapped an arm around her thin, shaking shoulders. "I know all this is pretty scary. Are you okay?"

A shrug lifted her arm.

"It's also hard to watch and not be able to do anything."

Marly sobbed in response.

"You can do what I do. Pray. God's there, listening, and He's with the boys, no matter what they've done. I'm going to pray for them. Want to join me?"

For a moment, Cate thought Marly would say no, but then she gave a quick nod. Well aware the teen wouldn't lead the prayer, Cate lifted the boys to the Lord, and at the end, she asked the Father to comfort Marly as well.

After their amens, she took Marly's hands in hers. "Do you need a ride home?"

"Oh, no! No. My dad…he's here. Volunteering with the Rotary Club. He'll get me home."

"You sure? I can take you now. You won't have to wait."

She shook her head. "I'll be fine. I'll go home with Dad."

Cate gave Marly a hug and then made her way toward her charges through a blur of emergency vehicles, EMTs, kids on cell phones and parents dragging curious youngsters away. Rotary Club members extinguished the bonfire. Cate gathered up the twins and Lindsay and with arms around them, huddled under the blanket for a moment. She wanted to head home, to get as far from this mess as possible, but she didn't want to leave Rand behind. For many reasons.

When the EMTs rolled the third gurney toward yet another ambulance, a grim-faced Rand nearly walked past her.

"Hey!" she called out.

"You're still here?"

"Well, I didn't want to strand you."

"I can catch a ride with one of the other guys. It's no big deal."

"It just didn't feel right, leaving you without saying anything. And your car's still at our house. Besides, I was worried about Phil and the two other boys." She watched the first ambulance pull out of the parking area, the red light swirling its alert. "I've never seen anything like that. Are they going to be all right?"

He shrugged and nodded toward the van. "Let's get going. I want to pick up my car and then head out to the hospital."

On the drive home, the twins were unusually quiet. Every glance Cate stole at the equally silent man in the seat beside her revealed a set jaw, eyes fixed on the road ahead and a tiny vein throbbing in his temple. She wished she could ask him to share his thoughts, but the closeness they'd shared on the hayride had vanished. She kept her peace.

Once in the driveway, Cate helped the kids out then called "Good night!" as Rand headed for his car. He stopped, turned and ran a hand over his face.

"Cate…I'm sorry." He looked up at the sky, then back at her. "I wish things were different. That I wasn't who I am, didn't have this job to do. I wish…I could just take you on your word. But I can't. It's not just about me. I need more. It's—"

"It's complicated."

He nodded.

She bit her bottom lip, then decided to take a chance. "I know what you mean. I—I care what you think. About me. And I want to prove to you I had nothing to do with any of this craziness. But I don't know what to do."

One broad shoulder rose and fell.

Cate's frustration grew. "I just wish this were all over. Now."

Instead of laughing at her Robby-and-Tommy-like outburst, Rand just nodded, confirming Cate's feeling that something had happened—changed—between them that night. Unfortunately, reality had jumped in again and interfered.

With a quiet "Goodbye" he turned and then got behind the wheel of his car. Still concerned about the soccer players, she wished she could go with him to the hospital, but she had no reason, no right to be there. She'd do better to take care of her trio and then pray for the teens.

An hour and a half later, when she turned off the lamp on her bedside table, she wondered what the morning would bring.

EIGHT

"Smurfs?" Rand asked. "What do blue cartoon characters from an old TV show have to do with skunk-drunk kids?"

The nurse who'd come out to speak with him gave him a humorless chuckle. "I wish it had something to do with Papa Smurf, or even underage drinking. Smurfs are pills with a silly nickname, but not so silly effects. They're a cheap substitute for ecstasy and some other hallucinatory drugs."

"What are the active chemicals?"

"Chemical. DXM—dextromethorphan. It's the main ingredient in cough syrup and other cold meds. The problem is its high toxicity at the quantity they take to achieve their high. You saw how sick it made them. It can and has led to death."

He ran a hand through his hair. "Are these guys going to make it?"

"Two of them look like they're going to be okay, but in a world of hurt for a few days, not to mention a ton of trouble."

"And the other boy?"

The nurse glanced toward the ER. "That old

cliché—time will tell. They're doing everything possible for him."

Anger filled Rand. "And you say the stuff's easily available?"

"What happens a lot of the time is that one kid will make a big buy on the Internet, then sell it off to his buddies."

Determination steeled Rand's spine. "We have to find out which one's doing the dealing."

Footsteps approached. "Welcome to my nightmare, Captain." Rand turned toward the newcomer. The tall, muscular man with his dark hair buzzed close to his head gave him a nod. "J.J. Colby, varsity soccer coach at Loganton High." The men shook hands. "We've got a growing problem in town and I'm having a time trying to keep up with the guys who're using."

"I hear it's not just the meth."

"Meth's not the first thing they try." The coach pointed toward a pair of armchairs and they sat. "They either outgrow the weed they start with or they get tired of the nasty side effects of the over-the-counter stuff pretty fast. That's the kind of thing these guys took and you can see the results."

"That's what I don't get. Who wants to go through that?" Rand's disgust grew. "I've never understood."

The coach ran a hand over his short hair. "I gotta tell you, with as hard as those guys work on the field, how much they train, the way they're so careful with their diet, I've never been able to understand how they can turn over control of their minds and bodies to this. Especially not Phil Britton and Dave Lawrence."

"What about the meth problem?"

The taut lines of the coach's posture screamed his frustration. "We've had a death and a near-miss at school. It's there and growing."

"You know about the fire and what we found at the theater, right?"

The coach nodded.

"I suspect you catch a lot of the buzz at school. What do you hear from the kids?"

"I hear plenty. Much of it is exaggerated or flat-out lies but unfortunately, some of it's true. The problem is, I don't have anything solid to take to my principal, much less the cops."

"Tell you what. You tell me what you're hearing and I'll track down the evidence." The coach hesitated. "I'm not in the business of busting high school boys— unless one of them's the ringleader of the meth operation that sent my boss and Wilma Tucker to the hospital and is poisoning your kids."

"No way. My guys...I don't think they're what anyone would consider real addicts. They're more along the lines of recreational users."

A ping alerted them to the just-arrived elevator. Alec Hollinger stepped out with several very upset parents.

"There you are, J.J.," the youth group leader said. "Phil Sr. and Rozie Britton wanted to thank you for giving them a call." When he spotted Rand, Alec gave him a narrow-eyed look. "Captain Mason. I didn't expect to see you here."

"I was at the bonfire when the boys began having trouble. Couldn't go to sleep without knowing how they're doing."

Phil Sr. stepped forward, hand outstretched. Rand

shook it. The distraught father cleared his throat. "I appreciate what you did. If you hadn't helped them, they could have passed out or even choked without anyone noticing." He swallowed hard. "If not for you, we might have been planning a funeral. As it is, David Lawrence's family doesn't know yet what they might have to face."

The image of Cate's horrified face flew into Rand's head. He couldn't take the credit due another. "You'll have to thank Cate Caldwell, the fire chief's daughter. She's the one who noticed the boys. She's the one responsible for saving their lives."

That was when the irony struck him. Years ago, Cate had played a part in two deaths. Now, she'd helped save two boys. And maybe, if things turned around, maybe even three.

From the depths of his Sunday School memories, a word bubbled up. It slugged Rand harder than if he'd taken a punch to the gut.

Redemption.

And it didn't come alone either. It came with another very potent word.

Repentance.

Was that what made Cate tick these days?

In the light of day and back in the office at the fire station, suspicion tried to bubble up again. True, it might all be coincidental, but in Rand's line of work, coincidence didn't exist. Trouble did.

Cate's history, Sam's return, the meth lab, the album, the photos and the love letter, the melted ID tag she found on the sidewalk, even her association with Phil Britton…

He'd noticed the hug she'd given the soccer star when she'd arrived at the hayride. And Cate had even told him she'd had Phil babysit before. Could she have given him something? From everything Rand had observed to date, Cate seemed clean. He'd not noticed anything in her demeanor, in her behavior, that would suggest drug use.

Others in town vouched for Cate, both personally and for her efforts with the kids. She could very well be as clean as she said she was. But still, Rand couldn't just ignore the coincidences. No matter how much, in spite of his better judgment, he wanted to.

He thought back to the night of the hayride, to what they'd told each other as they'd said their goodbyes. He'd admitted he wanted to believe her, but he couldn't, not without proof.

To his amazement, she'd responded by telling him she cared what he thought of her. And that she wanted to prove her innocence to him.

If only they were strangers, not bound by history or an arson investigation. Not to mention the intrusion of drugs into their reality.

But he couldn't discount the evidence. On the surface, it might not all add up to much, but taken within the context of the world of illegal drugs, it might mean more than first met the eye.

Sam could have come back to the awaiting Cate, who might have helped him set up the meth lab. She could have dropped the ID and then when she realized what had happened, brought it to Rand's attention. The photo album and love letter were self-explanatory once one accepted the possibility of an ongoing relationship between Cate and Sam during the past eight years.

And as far as the soccer team went, well, Cate could have been supplying them with their drug of choice—

No. He just couldn't see her dealing drugs. No matter what the evidence—and it was all circumstantial. He couldn't believe how Cate affected him. He'd never reacted to a person involved in one of his investigations like this. She was dangerous to his peace of mind. And maybe more.

It occurred to him his suspicion of Cate had more than one reason for being. True, circumstantial evidence linked her to Sam and the fire. But he couldn't deny his reluctance to care for her. She was unlike any other woman he'd ever met.

Was he using his suspicion as a way to keep her at arm's length? Was he that scared of falling for her?

There was something to be said for emotional safety—even if another term for it might be emotional cowardice. Was he that scared of falling for Cate Caldwell?

Or were his suspicions justified? How would they play out?

As he stared at the lists he'd made and turned his pen from tip to top over and over again, the two powerful words that had come to him the night before returned.

Repentance and redemption.

It was possible. They were two cornerstones of the faith Cate professed. Could they also be the keys to the change folks in town said she'd made?

Rand couldn't deny the inner lift he got at the thought of Cate being exactly who and what she said she was, nothing more, nothing less.

But for the words to be any kind of key, then there

really had to be power behind them. The God from whom Rand had walked away had to exist.

But if God was there, why did He not prevent more of the devastation one couldn't fail to see in the everyday world? Why did He leave His children to stumble along from disaster to disaster on their own? Why did He let decent people die as a result of others' wrongdoing?

Rand stood, pushed away from the desk and threw his pen down on the notepad. "Nope. Nothing's out there."

Not anything loving, compassionate, peace-giving. All one had to do was take a look at the mess the world was in.

The next Wednesday, Cate walked into the gym ten minutes before the youth group session started. A tough four days had passed since the bonfire. The soccer players had been suspended from school for a week, starting from when they'd recovered, and they'd been permanently removed from the team roster. Phil's future was forever altered.

David Lawrence, the boy who'd lost consciousness, remained in a coma, his future uncertain.

The whole episode made her heart ache. What a waste. A sense of urgency built up in Cate. How could she best help? How could she show kids they didn't need harmful substances to enjoy their social interactions? That all drug use accomplished was destruction and loss? That their concept of "partying" led only to devastation?

She looked around the vast room at the kids who'd arrived early. There were artists, musicians, teachers, lawyers, doctors, counselors, law enforcement officers in the making among them. The world needed these young people to make their marks. Cate wanted to prevent more loss, to help keep them busy, focused on serving Christ, bearing the fruit of their faith.

"Hi, Miss Cate."

She turned to see Hillary and two friends walk into the gym. "Did you ladies put together a list of blessings for the benefit? Any good ideas?"

The pretty blonde waved a notebook. "We've been brainstorming. This is soooooo cool..."

As they started toward the classroom Alec had assigned to Cate and her girls, the metal door opened and, to her surprise, Rand came in.

She sent the girls ahead. "Well, hello, there," she said. "I'm surprised to see you here."

Rand raised a shoulder. "After Saturday night, I figured I should do my part to help keep the town's kids from following in the footsteps of Phil and the others."

"Are you a member here?"

He glanced around the gym. "I suppose, because I never formally left the church, even when I moved."

But you left your faith.

Cate had no idea where the thought had come from, but she knew she'd hit the nail on the head. And she was glad she hadn't blurted out the words. Rand's spiritual condition was none of her business.

"Has Alec told you about Tuckerpalooza?" she asked.

"We got to talking Saturday night in the hospital waiting room. I figured I could lend a hand, especially with a hammer, to build booths. We've gotten so much done in the last few days—there's painting you and your girls can do."

Her heart thudded faster in her chest as he smiled

at her. Cate was sure her response had everything to do with the way Rand's gaze dived so deep, burrowed into what felt like the most private corners of her heart and stripped her feelings bare.

She hoped the smile she gave him looked more natural than it felt. "Welcome aboard. I'm sure the boys will be glad to have your help—I know Alec's probably doing an inner jig of joy now that he's roped in both of us."

As Cate walked toward her classroom and the gallons of paint the guys had stored there, she felt Rand's stare on a figurative target smack dab on her spine. Sure, he could stare all he wanted. The more he watched her, the sooner he would satisfy his curiosity—and put his suspicions to rest.

Then? Well, she'd have to trust God with the "then."

By the time Cate and the girls returned with the rollers and the paint, the gym floor had been covered with massive drop cloths, taped to the baseboards with bright blue painter's tape. The girls hovered around Cate, looking to her for direction.

Armed with a paint-laden roller, she went to work with the teens. The chatter in the background eased her nerves, still tense from when Alec called the group together and led them all in prayer, lifting Wilma, Joe and even Cate, Lindsay and the twins, to the Lord.

When Alec had mentioned her name, she'd again felt Rand's stare, intent and questioning. She'd sensed his discomfort at their prayer, but there'd been nothing she could do at that moment.

Next time they were alone…next time, she wouldn't

chicken out. And then, maybe, the strain between them would disappear once and for all.

Cate took a deep breath. Maybe…maybe that unexpected attraction she'd experienced from the start would grow into something stronger between them. She'd begun to catch glimpses of something other than his outward strength, his commitment to his work and his firm approach to right or wrong. Rand hid pain behind his rejection of God and maybe even his devotion to his job.

She began to wield her paint roller, a prayer in her heart. But then, a shriek cut through the hum of activity in the gym, and cries for help followed.

"Miss Cate!" Hillary called. "She just dropped. I don't…don't think she's breathing. Oh, please! Please help!"

Cate rushed to Hillary's side. There she found Marly had collapsed and lay sprawled on the drop cloth, her face white, her chest motionless.

Cate caught her breath, yanked out her phone.

Alec cleared the area around the fallen girl.

Cate dialed 9-1-1.

Rand dropped to his knees and began CPR. The rage on his face stabbed at Cate's heart.

She prayed until the operator answered.

The EMTs were sure Marly had overdosed, even though they didn't know what she'd taken. Toxicology would reveal all. But it didn't matter what they found. It wouldn't change a thing. Marly was gone.

Cate held the inconsolable Hillary until her parents arrived. "I didn't know she'd started using, Miss Cate."

Hillary's sobs echoed the pain in Cate's heart. "I promise. I didn't. Why would she have done that?"

The plaintive question echoed the pointed one Rand had asked Cate about her own walk on the dark edge of disaster. "All I can tell you is that I did some stupid things when I was her age and even now, I don't have a good answer to that question."

Hillary's parents arrived, and Cate murmured neutral responses when they thanked her for comforting their daughter at such a horrific time. But Cate knew she'd failed. Another teen had lost her life. This one, a "good girl" by all accounts and one Cate might have reached had she been able to intervene, to implement the drug awareness program.

She had plenty of ammunition against Alec's earlier argument. Passivity hadn't worked. Aggressive action couldn't do any worse and might do some good.

Rand came at her then, loaded, as usual, with a multitude of questions. He started right in. "What do you know about Marly Wooten?"

"Very little. I met her when I started helping with the youth group. I gave her a ride home that one night when her mother was busy."

"You do know her boyfriend."

"Her boyfriend?"

"Yes. Hillary says she'd been dating Phil Britton for about six weeks."

Oh, boy. Super-shy Marly and the soccer star. A bad combination. "I didn't know."

Rand mulled it over. "You didn't know they were dating, but you do know him. You told me you'd even had him watch Lindsay and the twins."

Cate couldn't miss the edge of reproach in his voice. "I never saw any sign of Phil's drug use before the hayride. And I would have recognized it. I had no reason to suspect him. And Marly? Her behavior didn't raise any flags during the times I worked with the youth group. She probably only used sporadically. Just like Phil."

Rand's detached expression left her wanting to reach out and shake him. Instead, she took a deep breath. "I'm going to talk to him, though. If for no other reason than that he has watched my kids and I have that connection with him. I want answers—"

"We've already talked to him."

So potential action did get a response. She'd threaten until she was blue in the face, if in the end they got somewhere. "I'm not official. Kids tend to back away from you guys."

He sighed. "And you would know."

She tipped up her chin. "Unfortunately."

"I hope you're not planning to go off on your own."

"I don't think you'll let me get away with it, will you?"

Rand shook his head. "If Hillary didn't know about Marly's drug use, it could have been something new. Maybe as new as her relationship with Phil. But we still don't know who sold the soccer players the drugs, much less Marly. We're on it, we're investigating."

Cate planted her fists on her hips. "I can help, you know. I can talk to Phil."

Rand studied her for a moment. "I'll be there with you. Marly was our witness. And we just learned the melted ID you found at the theater belonged to someone from the school—a kid, a teacher, a member of the staff." He took a deep breath. "And we don't know whether her death was an accident or something far worse. It may not be safe for you to get involved, any more than you already are."

On the way home, Lindsay and the twins started to belt out songs they'd sung in their respective groups. As they turned the corner to the Caldwell home, the trio hit their favorite chorus. They begged Cate to join in. And while she'd rather have spared them, she had to tell them about Marly. That put an end to the songs.

A familiar little yellow car blocked the driveway. Cate pulled onto the gravel on the side of the paved drive, parked, then rolled down her window.

"Zoe Ramona Donovan! What are you doing here at this hour of the night?"

The tall redhead unfurled her lean frame from its cramped spot behind the wheel of the subcompact. "I lead a boooooring life, sister. I have nowhere else to go—"

"That's your choice, Zoe. You use bug spray to keep the guys away."

"Yeah, well. You know I'm waiting for the right one to come around." She reached into the backseat and pulled out a tote bag. "I come bearing gifts—one gift, to be precise."

The kids opened the van doors and piled out.

"Whatcha got?"

"Who's it for?"

"Can I see, Miss Zoe?"

Cate clicked the van doors shut. With a glare at her

friend, she pointed her niece and nephews toward the front door. "It better not be alive, covered in fur, feathers, scales or slime. Or you're roadkill." She lowered her voice. "You know I can't handle a pet right now. And tonight's the worst possible night for one of your stunts. We…we had a death at youth group."

Zoe expressed her horror as Cate described the events of the evening. Before she knew it, she'd poured out everything: the attacks, the car that followed her home, the man at the window and even the album Sam had kept.

"I hope you understand," she said in the end. "I can't handle anything more."

Zoe tugged on her ponytail, a wry look on her face. "I hope you'll still love me after I show you my surprise. Plus remember, God's on your side, kiddo. Things might be horrible right now, but He's still on His throne."

"I know He is." Cate gave her friend a crooked grin—the best she could come up with. "Just show me what you brought my wild beasts. And it'll cost you. You're going to have to babysit my crew tomorrow, when the organizers for Tuckerpalooza come over for burgers and dogs."

"Oh, no!" Zoe winked at Lindsay who stood on the front porch straining to hear the adult conversation. "Dire consequences, indeed." She turned to the twins. "Psst! Hot fudge sundaes and banana splits for dinner!"

Cate shook her head and smiled. "So what did you bring them this time?"

Once inside the Caldwell living room, Zoe placed her tote bag on the coffee table in front of the sofa. The bag had mesh windows of the breathing-vent kind.

Cate groaned again.

Zoe unzipped the tote and out stumbled a tiny, marmalade-striped tabby kitten, its green eyes huge, triangle ears perked upright, its whiskers quivering. It blinked and sat, curled its tail around itself, then stared at Cate.

"Meeeow!"

Her wall of objections crumbled in the face of the perfect distraction.

The kids needed something positive after all the horrible stuff that had happened. While nothing could make up for Marly's loss, a kitten full of life and growing daily, bore the promise of hope.

"Awww…" Lindsay crooned.

"Is he gonna bring us dead rats?" Tommy asked.

Robby raced to the cat and picked it up. Yes, this was just what they needed.

NINE

"Don't worry about the firewood, Catey," her father insisted on the phone the next day. "I set it all up already. I've got someone coming to split it for you. Then the twins can help stack it for winter on the back porch."

"Dad! You didn't have to worry about firewood. You're supposed to be resting and recovering. I can take care of all that."

"You want me to just sit here and let my brain rot while I grow new skin?"

"No. I want you to get better."

"I'm doing that, too. But you can't make a guy watch TV all day. I tell you, it'll drive you nuts, with so many talk shows and people acting crazy."

Cate couldn't disagree, so she'd let it go.

Hours later, after she picked up the kids at school and hurried home, she sat to wait for the delivery of the felled tree her father had volunteered to take to help a buddy clear his property after a violent storm. And to keep the family warm once temperatures plunged.

When the doorbell rang, the kids pelted downstairs. The boys couldn't wait to try their hand at splitting logs—no matter how many times she told them they'd be getting near an ax only in their dreams. Lindsay held Crush—as in Orange Crush—in her arms, the kitty's happiness audible in his purring.

Cate hurried to the door. "Please put Crush back in his carrier. We're all going to be running in and out and I don't want him to slip away. He's little and can get lost or hurt if we aren't careful."

She opened the door. Rand stood on the other side. She couldn't help the smile that curved her lips.

"*You're* the one who lost the tree on your property?"

"No, I moved into a condo when I came back to town. Your dad just asked me to help, because he couldn't do it himself. I'm going to chop it down to size and get the boys to stack it for you."

"Don't expect me to just sip tea and nibble crumpets while you're at it. I want to do my part. Let's go stack wood."

Armed with a chainsaw, ax, sledgehammer and a wedge, Rand had the rough-cut wood dumped out of the truck onto the driveway. Before long, the saw hummed, its song punctuated in steady syncopation by the crack of the ax against the wood or the sledgehammer against the wedge.

The boys took the cut pieces from Rand, then raced each other to the back porch where the Caldwells had always stacked firewood for use in the winter. Cate took up a rake and started in on the thick layer of dead leaves, something she hadn't done since the fire. Lindsay helped her with her own small rake, sticking close by Cate's side.

The normalcy of their activity began to lull her into a state of contentment. This man, so at ease with himself and the kids, appealed to her as none other ever had before. He laughed, he answered the kids' questions, yet he never stopped working the whole time. When it came to correcting the kids or making any kind of decision, however, he made clear she was in charge.

Oh, yeah. She could really, really like this Rand. Admire him, relate to him…

Maybe even get answers from him.

Cate bided her time. She wanted nothing more than to ask about the investigation. What had he learned? Had the melted ID yielded any more information? Had his own investigation turned up anything to help the police nail whoever had put her dad and Wilma in the ICU?

But she couldn't just jump into the conversational mix between him and the twins—she wanted to spare her niece and nephews as much fear as possible. Talk of arson and arsonists wasn't particularly peaceful, and a discussion of the town's drug epidemic wouldn't be good for their peace of mind.

The boys kept Rand entertained, discussing soccer, school and their favorite video game. Lindsay slipped inside to play with Crush.

When Cate had built a tall pile of leaves for the town's services to pick up for disposal, she put away the rake and went to help Rand and the twins. From about a ten-foot distance, she paused to watch him, admiring the way his arms lifted the ax, then swung it back down in a smooth, powerful arc, his movements graceful in a rhythm all their own.

The man was impressive.

"Can I give it a try?" she asked.

"Why would you want to?" he grinned. "I'm right here."

"You won't always be available to chop our wood. I should know how to take care of us."

Rand crossed his hands on the wooden ax handle, leaned back and through narrowed eyes, took Cate's measure—again. This time though, a certain spark, a responding flicker, made Cate's heart beat faster.

Oh, my.

A flush warmed Cate's cheeks, but also served to warm her. She couldn't let him rattle her.

What had they been talking about? Oh, right. Chopping wood. But when Cate went to press her point, he stopped her. "Tell you what. If you show me you can swing a sledgehammer safely, I'll let you give the ax a try. At least the hammer won't chop off your foot."

"Your confidence in my ability overwhelms me," she said.

"You might be—" he took another look, a half-smile tipping up the corner of his mouth "—oh, about five foot seven, but you weigh next to nothing. It takes a certain bulk to handle one of these things. No reflection on you, of course."

Cate stuck out her chin. "I still want to give it a try."

His eyes twinkled. "Go for the hammer first."

"You go, Aunt Catey!" Robby cheered as he ran toward the house. "But wait until I get back from the bathroom."

Tommy frowned. "You sure you want to try, Aunt Cate? We don't want you in the hospital with Gramps."

He did have a point. She had to be careful. "Tell you what. I'll be really careful."

The back door slammed shut as Robby went inside, then immediately burst open again. Lindsay ran out, her face crumpled, a wail on her lips.

"Robby let Crush out! Someone get him, please!"

An orange blur dashed across the yard and into the shrubs between the Caldwell home and Alec's place. Tommy ran to the bushes and crawled under the greenery. Lindsay stood rooted to the back porch and stared, wringing her hands.

Cate headed for the driveway. "Okay, okay, okay. Wait right here while I go get Crush."

She trotted to the front, unlatched the gate on Alec's fence and hurried to the backyard. Behind her, Tommy lobbied Rand for permission to go after the kitten, too.

To her surprise, he backed her up. "Your aunt told you to stay here. How about if we get back to the wood?"

Alec's backyard was as neat as the front—not surprising, since he'd struck her from the start as a neat freak.

In the middle of the expanse of still-green lawn, Cate tried to settle on her best option. The faintest mewl from inside Alec's garage caught her attention. The old wooden door hung warped with a gap between its bottom edge and the concrete drive. Fortunately for Cate, it swung rather than rose up to open—no automatic garage gizmo to hinder her rescue efforts. She pulled on the creaky door and then once she had it ajar, waited while her eyes adjusted to the dark.

Seconds later, she saw the orderly garage, walls covered with floor-to-ceiling shelves. Vast quantities of stuff made the wooden boards sag under the weight, the full lower racks a perfect hiding place for a runaway kitten.

"C'mere, Crush. Let's get you home before you find a mouse trap or something."

The meow came again and Cate followed the sound to the rear wall. There, on a shelf stacked three deep with a dozen cans of drain-clearing lye, she found the cat huddled in a quivering heap. It seemed Crush's flight had scared him almost as much as he'd frightened Lindsay.

"Aw, sweet baby. Let's go home." As she stood up, she cracked her head against the next shelf up. One of a dozen gallons of antifreeze tumbled to the ground.

"Ouch!" Cate rubbed her head with one hand, while she clutched Crush to her chest with the other.

"What's up, Cate?" Alec asked, startling her. "You need something from my garage?"

Still checking her sore scalp, Cate held out the tiny bit of orange fur. "Alec Hollinger, meet the newest member of the Caldwell family. Crush ran away when one of the twins went inside to use the bathroom. I came after him before he could get into any kind of trouble here in your handyman's dream warehouse. Are you preparing for a siege or what?"

He barked a laugh. "I just like a bargain when I can get one. And it looks like you got your little buddy just in time. He's perfectly fine and a fine feline specimen at that." He rubbed between the kitten's perky ears as they left the garage. "I'm glad. But Crush's escapade tells me I'd better do something about that old door. I've been putting it off since I moved in. If he can slip in that way, then other critters can, too, and I have stuff that's not too healthy for them."

"Oh, I don't know. Maybe if the rats and squirrels get a whiff of your stuff, it'll keep them away."

Alec locked the garage door, then laughed at himself. "As if locking it does any good. Neither Crush nor the rats have to open the door to get in."

"No, but I'm glad I could. Otherwise, who knows if the poor little guy would have found his way back out."

"Well, there you go. It all worked out fine in the end."

"Tell that to the lump on my head." Alec laughed again. "See you later for the cookout," she added.

"Cookout?" Before she could remind him, he went on. "Oh, yeah. I almost forgot about that. Do you need any help? Want me to bring something?"

"Yeah. Bring whatever you signed up to bring, like everyone else. It's a potluck, Alec!" She shook her head. "Never mind. I think I have it all under control. Just bring your appetite."

When the twins and Rand had finished stacking the lumber on the back porch, Zoe drove up to collect the kids. While it took them a few minutes to load all their gear, the kitten and his litter box and all kinds of odds and ends into her friend's zippy little car, before long, Cate felt a brief measure of relief.

Then she turned to Rand as they headed into the kitchen. "I refuse to accept 'nothing' as an answer this time. Bring me up to date. What have you learned about the fire so far?"

"I really don't have anything more to tell you about the fire. We're waiting for lab results on additional tests they've run."

"But…?"

He sighed. "Taken up mind-reading lately?"

"No. Just years of watching Dad as he worked fires. I can tell when you guys have something else itching at your minds."

He sighed. "It's about the soccer players. The third boy said David didn't buy the drugs off the Internet."

Cate's thoughts spun in a dozen directions. "Then that means someone's dealing at the school. Did any of them say who it was?"

Rand shook his head. "They refused to talk. Which tells me they're scared. I don't think it's another kid."

A sick feeling swam into Cate's gut. She looked at the platter of burgers she held. She didn't know if she'd be able to cook them without getting sick.

"This is bad, really bad."

"Yeah, it's bad."

"Related to the meth?"

"I don't know. But I wouldn't be surprised. Dealers aren't too picky about how they make their dough. And pills are easy to come by."

"Could it have been Sam? Before he died, I mean."

"Could be, but even though we found a backpack, some clothes and your album, we found no money at all. Makes me doubt he had the funds to set himself back up in business."

"That means someone supplied him with the ingredients to cook up the drug."

"Either that or Sam was little more than an errand boy for the real dealer. We checked with the jail. He'd been out for only two weeks. It seems he came straight to Loganton the minute he got out."

"He didn't come to me, Rand. I hadn't seen him."

The look he gave her made her feel like they'd gone back to square one.

She didn't let him speak. "What good would it do me to lie? I don't have the money to fund a meth lab nor do I have the kind of profit a lab would turn. You can check that out easy enough. Subpoena my bank records, if you insist on suspecting me."

He arched a brow. "I might just do that, Cate."

She made herself take measured steps as she went out to the back porch and slapped eight burgers on the hot grill.

Seconds later, she heard Rand come out on to the porch, but she didn't turn. Why did this man throw her so off balance? Cate had felt the same way back in high school. Back then, she'd chalked up her awareness to resentment. Her father had considered Rand almost perfect, while Cate never quite hit the mark.

Cate felt Rand's warm hands lightly grasp her shoulders, and then his low voice rumbled in her ears, interrupting her thoughts.

"Look, Cate. I know it's tough to deal with, but I do have a job to do. I'm accountable to Loganton. It's my responsibility to suspect everyone." He sighed. "But don't worry. You have nothing to fear from me. I believe you, Cate."

And then he deliberately leaned forward to press a kiss on her forehead. The sweetness of it sent her senses reeling. Slowly, she smiled as he turned and went back inside.

The cookout was great. Everyone came prepared and the committees gelled almost on their own. True, everyone had plenty of experience with the Fall Fest and they all assumed their same responsibilities as for the seasonal event. Still, many odds and ends needed attention beyond those obvious necessities and people stepped up to the plate.

Coach Colby took over the games. His wife, Abby, chose to coordinate the arts and crafts sales booths. Maggie Reams, the pastor's wife, would chair the bake sale, and Gail Sowers, the new church secretary and librarian, would gather donations for the book sale. The eight Sunday School teachers volunteered in one capacity or another, while Alec, Cate and Rand agreed to coordinate the entire event.

At nine-thirty, Cate hit overload and began to fade. Folks packed up to leave, their now-empty food containers washed and dried by the efficient Alec and his kitchen minions. He'd marshaled the cleanup from the start.

"It's the least I can do," he'd said. "I've roped all of you into this madness. I owe you."

From her vantage point in the middle of the kitchen, she could see not a speck of sauce, not a potato peel, not a cup or spoon out of place. "Thank you so much," she told Alec. "Everything's better than when you got here."

"I aim to please, ma'am. Besides, Beth's got me well trained. She'd kill me—or at least yell my ear off when I call to say good night—if she heard I didn't clean your kitchen to her meticulous standards."

Cate laughed. "You're a neat freak yourself and you can't deny it, Alec. So don't blame your poor pregnant wife."

"Hey! I like peace in my life. If clean's what Beth wants, clean's what Beth gets."

Abby elbowed her husband. "Did you hear that? Let's see if you can pick up some pointers, buster."

The coach grumbled, but wore an ear-to-ear grin.

Finally, Rand and Alec were the only ones left. Rand waved a sheaf of papers. "We got a lot done. Are you busy tomorrow afternoon? Want to go over—"

A buzzing cut him off. He reached into his pocket and pulled out his phone. Moments later, a frown lined his brow and he slapped the phone shut. "Sorry, guys. Fire out on Ardmore Road. I should go."

As Rand gathered his tools, Alec took off the apron he'd borrowed, then stepped back into the kitchen to hang it on a hook by the door. Back in the living room moments later, he nodded to Cate. "I'll see you tomorrow."

Finally, Rand stood alone in the living room, ax, wedge and chainsaw in hand, a somewhat reluctant expression on his face. Cate couldn't figure out why he hadn't already bolted.

"Thank you so much for your help. And I still want that wood splitting lesson."

He groaned.

Cate chuckled. "Oh, go keep your men in line."

"Actually, they know what they're doing. Your father's a fine chief. He has them well-trained. I hardly have to do anything, but it is my job. Will you be okay? You look exhausted."

She leaned against the doorframe, her every muscle tired, her head swimming, a faint wooziness threatening to drop her to the ground. "It has been a long day—

a long couple of weeks. I think I'll crash for a while on the couch in the living room. At least, until the end of the news."

Rand glanced at the TV set, then back at Cate, his voice gentle, his expression concerned. "Make sure you do go to bed, though. Otherwise, you might wake up in worse shape than when you started out."

"I'll be fine. Thanks again."

Cate locked the door behind Rand. Silence echoed throughout the house—unusual, since the walls usually rang with the sounds of life. She missed the kids. But she would never have accomplished anything for the benefit fund-raiser had Lindsay and the twins been around.

She wandered back to the living room, clicked on the TV and turned the volume to low, then grabbed her Bible and turned to the Psalms. Fifteen minutes later, she realized she hadn't focused at all. She was tired, sleepy, that strange lightheadedness still with her, worse than before. And it didn't help that her thoughts keep turning to Rand. And that kiss.

And the lack of a goodbye kiss. What was up with that?

Was Rand doing good cop, bad cop—all-in-one arson investigator? Or had they really made progress?

Cate yawned, then scootched down lower on the couch until she lay curled under the cozy chocolate wool throw, her head on the tapestry pillow her mother had made years ago.

If Rand spent more time working with her instead of against her, being nice instead of suspicious, she would find herself losing her head…her heart.

If things continued down this path, she might find herself in love with the man she'd seen today, trusting the man who'd helped chop wood, who hadn't talked down to the twins, who'd pitched in and helped plan a fund-raiser. This was a man with whom she could spend time, one with whom she could share her life.

This was a man she could love. For the rest of her life…

She yawned again, exhaustion overpowering her, unable to fight the stranger slumber that lured her ever more seductively by the minute. Her eyes closed, almost against her will.

Whoever had thought setting fire to a pile of leaves on the side of a country road was a good idea deserved to have their hair singed off. The blaze had come dangerously close to the Hodges' farmhouse. The family might have been hurt or killed had they not been late picking up the kids from the sitter after the parent-teacher conferences the parents had attended at the middle school.

Now, Rand wanted nothing more than a shower and his bed. In that order. And with no distractions.

But then his phone rang. It was Joe Caldwell, who should have been asleep in his hospital bed.

"What's up?" Rand said in greeting.

"I'm not sure, son. I tried calling Catey, but she's not answering. That girl never lets the phone ring like that."

"She's probably sleeping. When I left the house about an hour ago, she said she was going to lie down in the living room to watch the news before heading to bed. I warned her she might sleep through the night there if she wasn't careful. She probably didn't hear your call."

"I'm telling you, Rand. That doesn't sound like her. A pin falls and she wakes up. She's always been like that, ever since she was little."

"Tell you what. I'll run by the house and check on her on my way home. We just had a little incident out on Ardmore, at the Hodges' place. I'll have her call you so you can rest easy and go back to sleep."

"Sounds good." The relief in Joe's voice was palpable. "Sorry to bother you like this, but you'll understand the day you have yourself a couple of kids of your own."

Rand laughed. "Hey, at the rate I'm going, looks like I'll be passing on that mixed pleasure."

"Nah, you won't. There's a girl out there somewhere, just right for you. You're going to have to quit working so many hours to let her find you, though."

Rand instantly thought of Cate. "Bite your tongue, Boss. My life doesn't need that kind of complication at this time."

"Aw, go on. Go check on Catey. And get yourself some rest."

"I'll try. See you tomorrow."

Ten minutes later, he drove up to the large white house again. When he saw the living room lights still on, an odd feeling came over him. The news had ended a while earlier. Had Cate just slept through the broadcast?

He went to the door and rang the bell.

No response. In the background, the murmur of the TV spoke volumes. He rang again, longer and with greater insistence this time.

With the same result.

And that's when he smelled it. A peculiar, rotten-egg smell.

Gas!

He fisted his hand, pounded on the door, called out her name.

Nothing.

He ran to the window three feet from the door. Through the filmy white sheers, he could make out the flickering lights of the TV, the couch and, under a blanket, Cate curled up, fast asleep.

He hoped.

The smell grew stronger.

He flipped open his phone and dialed 9-1-1. While it rang, he kicked in the glass. Cate didn't move. Carefully, he broke out the jagged shards that remained on the window frame as he gave the dispatcher the details.

Cate needed him.

He crawled through the window, not even pausing when a sliver of glass scratched his skin. "Cate!"

She didn't move.

Heart in his throat, he ran to the couch, scooped his arms under her slight frame and brought her up close. She was warm and while he could still feel her breathing, it was uneven, labored, a struggle to draw in life-giving air.

Had he gotten to her soon enough?

"Please! Please, please, *please!*"

He ran and didn't bother to open the door, giving it the same treatment he'd given the window, and burst into the night air. Insurance would pay for his sins.

He could focus only on the precious woman in his arms. And the need to know what—or who—had caused the deadly gas leak in her home.

TEN

Four hours later, after the gas company had turned off the supply to the Caldwell home and he'd had Cate rushed to the ER, Rand sat in the uncomfortable brown armchair in Cate's hospital room and watched her sleep. He'd ridden the ambulance to the ER and his guilt had grown with every mile the vehicle covered.

If there was one thing he'd learned about Cate Caldwell since he'd come back to town, it was that she loved her father, Lindsay and the twins. She'd never do anything to hurt them. How could he have thought she was behind all this?

Someone had tried to hurt—kill—Cate. His instincts practically screamed it at him.

A representative from the gas company had stayed behind at the Caldwell house to go over every inch of the gas-delivery system. Soon enough, Rand would know where the leak had originated. Until then, he wasn't letting Cate out of his sight. It was the least he owed Joe.

And Cate herself.

He couldn't help but wonder if his suspicions might have pointed the wrong someone's attention her way. If that was the case, how would Rand atone for the harm he'd unwittingly caused her—a woman he admired, a woman he cared for, a woman he was coming to love?

"You asked us to call you as soon as we found the leak," the gas company representative told Rand an hour later. "It was nothing more than a burner on the stove. It was left on, but the flame had gone out. From where we're standing, it looks like a careless mistake."

Rand weighed the man's words. "A careless mistake…"

"Happens more often than you might think, Captain. And the Caldwell's stove is old. Perfectly usable, you understand, but it is old and maybe the knob didn't twist all the way off."

Or someone intentionally didn't twist it all the way. Plenty of possible culprits had been through that kitchen earlier that night.

"Thanks for the call," Rand said.

After he hung up, Rand held the phone in his hand, weighing his options. He could call Hal or Ethan, but what were the chances either one would have checked the stove for fingerprints? Twenty or so sets would have shown up after the cookout, including Rand's.

On the other hand, the cleanup crew had scoured every inch of the kitchen before calling it a night. Could someone have wiped down the stove to remove evidence of tampering?

Sure. Someone could have done just that. But who would have done it? And why would they have targeted Cate?

The only possible reason was the drugs. Did she

know more than she realized about the drug culture in Loganton? Could she somehow connect the three soccer players and their supplier? Had she seen anything that might identify the person who'd set up Sam's operation in the theater's basement?

Or, as Rand feared, had his presence at her side alarmed the culprit? Had the dealer worried she might reveal his identity just by answering any of Rand's pertinent questions?

Rand glanced at the too-still figure on the bed. Cate looked sweet, young, incapable of committing a crime. He again felt guilty for doubting her and worried that he'd become as jaded as he'd feared after years of living in the mire of crime. He'd seen evil where evil didn't exist and wasted valuable time. And now Cate was in a hospital fighting for her life.

Could he ever forgive himself? Could she?

Cate awoke to a sore throat, a weird chemical taste in her mouth and an encompassing sense of disorientation. It took her a few minutes to get her bearings, to clear the dizziness and remember what had happened. All at once, the memories slammed back with full force.

She'd been exhausted—or so she'd thought. It turned out, according to the ER doctor who'd woken her with questions and tests, she'd come close to asphyxiating because of a natural gas leak in the house. The doctor said her father had tried to call to say goodnight and when she hadn't answered the phone, he'd turned to Rand. Rand had come over, pulled a swashbuckling hero stunt and saved her life.

She wished she'd been awake to see that.

Now here she lay in a hospital room, leashed by an IV to the metal-railed bed, her body sore and even more tired than she'd been on the couch at home. She squirmed, looking around the small room, and her gaze landed on the man uncomfortably scrunched into the pleather-covered armchair by the window.

Rand had fallen asleep, although Cate had to wonder how he'd managed that. His long frame sprawled mostly off the chair, his neck twisted to one side, his head drooped onto the ridge of the chair's back. He'd crossed his arms over his broad chest and he'd propped his ankles on a small trash can.

Deep emotion moved her. She would never forget the sight of him there, just as she'd never forget he'd saved her life.

As she studied his handsome features, he stirred. His blue eyes opened and before she could look away, he caught her studying him. For once, she didn't chicken out. She stared right back.

And while she couldn't quite describe what happened much less what caused it, something changed between them right then. Nothing would ever be the same.

Unspoken feelings, emotions not yet understood or accepted, the recognition of what might yet come to be. The stark hospital room shimmered with promise. Cate's heart took hope.

There was probably some truth to the old saying that a person who saved another owned a small bit of that rescued life. This was now personal, between her and Rand—between a man and a woman. She knew she could trust him with her life.

* * *

Once Cate went back to sleep, Rand let himself relax again. He'd woken up to find her staring at him, those rich brown eyes warm, questioning, inviting…something.

He'd wanted to respond, to reach out to her, to acknowledge what existed between them.

As strange as it was, he knew things had changed. Maybe his recognition of the likelihood of her innocence had freed him to experience his emotions, to accept evidence of hers. He didn't know for sure.

But he knew he couldn't walk away unless Cate was safe. Until he knew no one wanted to do her harm. Until he could prove to anyone and everyone she'd had nothing to do with Sam Burns's meth lab.

Yes, he wanted to prove her innocence rather than guilt. An unusual position to be in because he'd always wanted nothing more than to find the truth. This time, he wanted the truth to be all about Cate's innocence.

Rand sighed, stood and stretched his arms almost to the ceiling. He'd never slept in a more uncomfortable position, but it was all for a good cause. With another glance at Cate, he turned and slipped inside the small bathroom behind his miserable chair.

Minutes later, as he washed his hands, a strange sound in Cate's room startled him. A muffled groan, a rustle of fabric.

He yanked open the door and the sight that met his eyes shocked him.

The dark-clad intruder leaning over the bed, holding a pillow over Cate's face, bolted. Rand followed.

He had all the answers he needed.

As Rand raced after Cate's would-be killer, they sped past the nurses' station and the stern woman at the computer cried out.

"Gentlemen!" She stood and glared. "Stop! You can't run."

"Call the police!" Rand yelled over his shoulder, intent on catching his black-hooded prey. "He tried to smother Cate Caldwell. Check on her!"

When he turned the corner, the door to the stairs closed with a soft slap. He yanked it open, but found the landing empty. The intruder's footsteps echoed in the stairwell as he pelted down. Rand tore after the man, but his heart remained up in Cate's room. In the second before the killer had left, he'd seen Cate's struggle against the smothering pillow.

She'd be fine.

He'd probably scared off the person before any harm was done.

Probably.

A handful of floors down, he heard a door open and close again. The attacker had fled to the hospital's main lobby, where there were sure to be other people, even at this hour, people with whom the killer could blend in. He would likely disappear in plain sight. With nothing more than a flick of a hand to drop the hood from his face, the black sweatshirt would no longer make him stand out. Rand couldn't just accuse anyone wearing a dark top.

Frustrated, he noticed that no one seemed hurried, much less in mid-flight. Either Cate's attacker had blended in with the folks in the lobby, or he had gone straight to the door and left in the handful of seconds it had taken Rand to exit the stairwell. At this point, it would be useless to try and identify the perp. He'd have to wait and see if the hospital's surveillance cameras had caught anything more than the dark blur Rand had seen.

What were the chances the cameras had caught features obscured by the hood the man had worn?

Rand struggled with the urge to catch the guy and punish him with a well-placed fist. But that urge separated a professional from the criminals he caught. He'd be far better off doing his job, investigating, gathering evidence.

And protecting Cate.

He turned back and slipped into the elevator again. He punched the button on the illuminated panel, waited until the doors slid shut and then leaned against the back wall, his mind spinning without pause.

He would catch Cate's attacker. He had no doubt.

Fear. The real thing.

Cate had never experienced anything like it before. In the span of a couple of short weeks, however, she'd learned what it truly meant. And she didn't like it. Not one bit.

First, she'd feared for her father's life as she'd faced the raging inferno at the theater. And now, just minutes ago, she'd thought she was drawing her last breath. Her first thought had been of her niece and nephews. The kids needed her, especially with Dad still in the hospital, only now starting down the path of recovery from his injuries.

Her only other thought had been of Rand. She'd never have the chance to tell him how she truly felt about him…

Now, as grateful as she was to still draw breath, a number of questions grew more insistent by the minute. Cate wanted to know whose greediness would curse misguided kids to a life of addiction in order to line his pockets. And who had so much against her that he'd try to smother her?

She didn't want to die, even though she was ready to meet her Heavenly Father on His terms and at His time. But Cate didn't think this was the right time. She still felt needed here. So she'd fought off her attacker with her every ounce of strength. To her relief, Rand had burst in like an avenging angel, screaming and threatening her would-be killer just as she thought her lungs would explode. The man had fled the room with Rand in pursuit.

Moments later, the nurse had rushed in. By then, Cate had regained her breath. She'd surprised the woman with her anger, yelling for security and for the PD to be notified.

"Lord?" she'd said when the nurse had left. "I'm not strong enough to fight off that guy all on my own. I'm glad you sent Rand to help. But he won't always be waiting in the shadows. I'm going to need your strength, so please hold me up…"

Peace settled upon her, even though her temper still roared. So this was righteous anger.

The door to her room opened and a tall shadow fell across the foot of her bed. It had to mean something that she knew right away who it belonged to.

And that knowledge brought her unexpected comfort.

"I'm glad you're back," she said. "Did you catch him?"

He placed gentle fingers against her cheek, smoothed them down to her jaw line, dropped his hand to her shoulder and finally took her hand in his. "Are you okay? Did he hurt you?"

She squeezed that solid and sturdy hand gaining strength from his confidence and grit. "I'll be fine. Did you catch the guy?"

By the moonlight coming in through the window, Cate could see Rand's frustration etch tiny lines at the corners of his eyes. "By the time I got down to the main floor, he'd either mixed in with the people in the waiting room or left the building altogether."

With her free hand, Cate turned on the fixture over her head. The sickly fluorescent light gave Rand a haggard look. She couldn't miss the strain on his every feature.

"So what's the plan? What are you going to do to find him?" Her own frustration grew and she withdrew her hand from his clasp. "Are you going to follow the same plan you've used to investigate the fire? Are you going to tell me you're waiting for lab results and then accuse me of dealing drugs?"

He glared, but she didn't want to hear more vague nothings right then. "Don't try, Rand. I didn't hold that pillow over my own face. I didn't lay here *and* run out of this room at the same time."

"I never said you did—"

"You wasted time suspecting me when you should have been trying to find the real culprit."

"I *have* been—"

"Someone's selling drugs to kids. My niece and

nephews have been in danger of losing both my dad and me—and I don't even know why this creep's after me!"

The strain of all that had happened suddenly caught up with her, drained her and left her unable to continue.

Rand took advantage of her silence. "Cate. Please believe me. I'm on your side. Maybe later than you would have wanted me to get on board, but I know what's been happening. This guy has proven he's capable of anything. We'll catch him and take care of it."

She didn't try to stop the snort. "You aren't going to stop me from doing everything I can to protect my family—or myself. And learning who tried to kill me is part of that. It's time I got more involved with this investigation."

"I can't stop you from putting yourself in danger, but please think of the officers whose lives you'd risk."

He did have a point. Still… "Why haven't you caught the drug dealer yet?"

He ran a hand through his dark hair, rumpling it even more. This Rand, tired, frustrated, thwarted by the man who'd tried to kill her, struck her as more accessible, somehow more human than before. Maybe she could persuade him to see things her way.

He leaned over the bedside rail. "You don't think it's weighing on me? You don't think I want him locked away, so he can't do any more harm? So that he can't hurt you again?"

She didn't answer.

Rand's blues eyes blazed with determination. "I can't let you go out and get yourself killed. Next time he comes after you, I might not be behind door number one to chase him away. If you insist on playing TV sleuth, I'll have to alert both Ethan and Hal to your plans."

She stuck out her chin. "And you figure they're going to spend their days glued to me? I don't think so."

He crossed his arms. "Maybe I'm the one who's going to do that."

Cate studied Rand's posture. The man meant business. But she had no intention of backing down.

"I have a suggestion." That caught his attention. "What if we join forces? I know everyone in town. You've just come back. It's going to take you some time to get up to speed with Loganton and its residents."

"Are you telling me now you hobnob with drug dealers?"

She rolled her eyes. "Of course, not. And I'm pretty sure you're smart enough to have figured out that the guy who tried to kill me isn't exactly my buddy."

"True, but I don't see where your familiarity with the area is going to help. Whoever's behind all this isn't going to start wearing a sign that says, 'Catch me if you can.'"

"Of course he's not. But I know the kids and can ask questions. Before you bring it up, yes, I can be discreet."

"I'm not sure about this…"

"But I am. And I get a say in my life."

"While the best I can do is chase you around and try to keep you in one piece."

"Something like that."

"What about Lindsay and the boys?"

"This is one time when being in the hospital is a plus. I can let the neighbors know I'm recovering and the kids can stay with Zoe until it's safe to come home.

I'll have to sacrifice some time with them to make sure they have a future. I'll sneak in a visit here and there, but it's more important to keep them safe."

Cate yawned and a flash of guilt crossed Rand's face. He ran his hand through his hair again.

"I'm sorry. I've overstayed. You need to get your rest."

She shrugged. "I don't think I would be here to argue if you hadn't hung around long enough to scare off that guy."

He arched a brow. "So you do have some use for me, after all."

She blushed. "Brawn meets brain."

"And so the brain tells you not to try anything crazy without me, right?"

"Depends on what you call crazy. To me, crazy is sitting around waiting for this guy to come at me again."

"Just promise you won't do anything alone."

Cate suspected this was the best bargain she was going to strike. "Okay. I'll see you tomorrow, so we can plan our next step."

"You're big on planning."

She laughed. "Are you on board for tomorrow's planning session or not?"

"Don't suppose I can talk you out of it, so, yes. We're on for tomorrow's planning session." At her relieved smile, he went on. "Now go to sleep. You're going to need your rest."

She nodded, not wanting to push her luck.

Before she knew what was coming, he'd pressed his lips to hers for a short, sweet startling kiss that left her wanting more.

She watched him leave, her heart pounding.

Chalk one up for Loganton's fire department captain. He'd left her speechless—again.

But she could also chalk one up for her. She'd survived long enough to win Rand over to her side. Maybe now she'd get a few answers.

And catch a determined killer. Before he struck again.

ELEVEN

Rand made his way to the lounge on Cate's floor. The coffee machine would be his most stalwart companion through the dark hours. It was going to be a long night.

Ethan picked up on the first ring. "You're where?"

"The waiting lounge outside Cate's hospital room. Someone tried to smother her and I chased him away. Unfortunately, he was too fast for me. You'll want to come and check the surveillance video, even though I doubt you'll get anything."

"Isn't that the truth? We don't have much of anything to go on in this case."

"I know. But how about the ID Cate found? Anything new on that?"

"Now that you mention it, we do have something. The first three numbers on the bar code show it belongs to someone from the high school."

"The high school? You're telling me a kid might have torched the theater?"

"Not necessarily. The bar code's first three numbers are the same for teachers, students, staff, even maintenance workers. We were lucky to find that much. The plastic was very badly damaged."

"And our witness was a student, one who died of an overdose."

"Yes, she was."

"Hmm…"

"Don't get carried away with that thought, Rand. I don't think Marly was involved with the lab."

"The question is whether the ID has anything to do with the fire. Just like the person Marly saw outside the theater could have been there innocently, the card could have been dropped innocently."

"That's my point."

"But my gut tells me otherwise."

"If your gut leads you somewhere, then we can talk. In the meantime, I'll come over there to check things out. Hang tight, call Hal and I'll see you both in a while."

Rand dragged two armchairs together and stretched out to wait out the hours. He was here to stay and he had no choice but to forgo sleep. No way was he about to leave Cate unprotected.

If he'd left before, the killer would have succeeded.

Cate would have died.

Had it happened, he never could have lived with himself. He could no longer envision living without her.

Two days after she wound up in the hospital, the Saturday before Thanksgiving, Cate found herself wandering the empty house. It echoed with silence because she'd refused to have the kids home with her. She certainly wasn't about to put her niece and nephews in the killer's way.

With the approaching holidays, she'd decided to

decorate on her own and surprise the kids when they came back from Zoe's.

But now that the time had come to sort the decorations, Cate felt lonely. She hadn't expected how much she would miss Lindsay and the twins and all the lively fun that came with them.

She brought down the plastic tubs full of Christmas decorations, then spread out the contents over the living room sofa, the coffee table and the rug in the center of the room.

On top of missing Lindsay and the twins, as soon as Cate brought out the ornaments, she began to revisit the tough memories the holidays always brought back. While the pain had settled to a dull ache over the years, the loss of her sister came back as a sharp stab at Thanksgiving. Growing up, Cate had loved the holiday. The scents, the flavors, the abundance, the family gathering…it had all been wonderful as a child.

Then she'd spun off track. For a while, she'd avoided family times as though they'd rivaled root canals. Truth was, she'd known in her heart her actions were wrong. But she'd still done everything to avoid her parents. She'd known she was hurting them, but something burned inside her, propelled her to do what she'd been warned against.

Rebellion. A simple word. An ugly truth.

The doorbell rang. Cate dropped the tangled tree lights on the recliner and hurried to answer. To her surprise, Rand, Alec, J.J. and Abby stood on her front porch.

"You said you wanted to decorate," Rand said, giving Cate's shoulder a gentle squeeze.

A zing of anticipation rushed through her and the

warmth of joy filled her heart. Another day they'd spend together. "You shouldn't have. I know how busy you are. I can handle it."

He rolled his eyes. "I'm sure you can. I just don't think you should try to do it all on your own so soon after you broke out of the hospital. But I'm getting to know you better than you think." He stepped aside to let the others into the house. "I brought the troops."

Alec waggled a scolding finger at Cate. "You should have called me. You know I'm always there for you, Joe and the kids."

"I can't believe you guys are all here. I'm just sorting out the stuff. I haven't started anything, really."

J.J. looped an arm around Alec's shoulders. "Sounds like we're just in time. Give us the outside lights and we'll have the place looking like a magazine spread before you know it."

Abby pulled a notepad from her purse as the two men lugged a box out the front door. "I'm on my way to the store—I need more tinsel and a new tree skirt. Tell me what I can pick up for you."

As soon as Abby and Cate had finished a short list, Rand grabbed the tangle of tree lights. "This is my forte. Where's your tree?"

Cate shrugged, looked away. "Don't have one yet. I usually take the kids to cut one down outside of town."

His expression mellowed. "You miss them, don't you?"

"You have no idea." She drew a deep breath. "And it's not just them. True, I talk to Dad a couple of times a day, but it's not the same. The house is just not home like this. I…Thanksgiving—well, it's almost here, too."

A muscle tightened in Rand's cheek. "Yeah. Well. It comes every year."

She placed a hand on his forearm. "But it doesn't get any easier, does it?"

To her surprise, the big man's reaction was as heartfelt as her own. He covered her fingers, swallowed hard, then nodded. "It's tough, no matter what. Talking to Joe each year has helped."

"I didn't know you guys did that."

"He's the only one who understands."

"I understand."

His eyes graced her with a gentle look as he slid his fingers between hers. "I suppose you do know it's not all about turkeys and trees and garlands and carols and toys."

She nodded, tears in her eyes. "It's about family and love, but the traditions do help. That's why I try to make it a Christmasy Christmas every year. It's the least I can do for Mandy's kids."

When she mentioned her sister, Rand nodded, stepped back, cleared his throat and squared his shoulders. "Then what are we waiting for? I still have the chainsaw in the back of my SUV. Let's go hunt us a tree."

Disappointment struck as he put a little distance between them. And that surprised Cate. It had been a long time since she'd let anyone get close. And certainly, she'd never let any other man see that clearly into her pain.

Maybe busyness was for the best.

Forty-five minutes later, they hopped out of Rand's silver SUV and walked down the first row of pines. The afternoon crackled with bright fall sunlight, the sky blazed blue above, and the spicy scent of the trees had Cate feeling holiday excitement for the first time that year.

She and Rand tromped up and down the leaf-covered paths, their feet crunching the dried leaves on the ground, laughing at trees with crooked trunks, shunning those specimens with bare bellies, each lobbying for his or her favorite, finally narrowing the possibilities down to three beautiful evergreens.

In all the years she'd known him, she'd never seen Rand so relaxed or felt so at ease in his company. She could get used to this—she really wanted to get used to it. And hoped he did as well.

"Have you noticed," Rand said as he rubbed his chin, "that you have a Papa Bear, Mama Bear and Baby Bear kind of choice?"

Cate stood back and studied the three trees. They stood in adjacent rows and she couldn't decide which way to go. "Oh, you choose. God did all the hard work. He grew the beautiful trees, so you can't make a mistake, whichever one you pick."

Rand's smile vanished and his features took on a strain. She'd noticed his discomfort with any mention of God before, but she'd just spoken spontaneously, without a thought to his reaction. She hadn't considered what she'd said controversial. She wondered if he'd comment.

"The kids wouldn't like the small one—too small." His voice came out clipped from between tight lips. His eyes had grown cold. "And I think the biggest is too big. The middle one should work best."

Cate's enjoyment in the day disappeared with the change in Rand's attitude. "That's fine."

But it wasn't. His discomfort with her statement of faith stole her pleasure from the preparations for one of Christendom's greatest celebrations. And she knew Rand hadn't always felt that way about faith. She remembered him as the confident student council president and one of the leaders in the church's youth group years ago.

Why had he turned his back on God?

A Christmas tree chopping excursion didn't strike her as the right time to ask, but how would she know the right time when it came? If it ever did come. She wasn't likely to forget Rand's reaction; she couldn't. Cate knew what a comfort her Savior offered and in Rand's line of work, she knew he had and would experience much that would cause pain. The kind of comfort he would need could come only from a loving God.

She would pray for Rand. And if the right time did come, she would share with him how her faith had seen her through the darkest of nights.

They returned home in strained silence. Cate got the sense Rand wanted to say something, but she also got the feeling he was holding himself under strict control again.

Did her faith threaten him that much? What had happened to him?

By five, he'd coiled all the tiny white lights around the tree. Cate had separated the ornaments by color and had decided on a classic red, green and gold scheme for this year. She had enough decorations to deck out three trees in different schemes, but rather than an icy and elegant silver and blue, or her mother's off-beat and unique purple and gold, she'd decided comfort and tradition would suit everyone after all that had happened.

"Are you well enough to go to Marly's funeral tomorrow?" Rand suddenly asked after he'd plugged in the lights.

"I'm fine, Rand. I plan to go to church. I couldn't miss the funeral."

"I can give you a ride."

Was Rand holding out the olive branch? Or just acting as her bodyguard?

Cate bit her bottom lip. She'd thought their relationship had reached a new level after he'd saved her life. That kiss… And just a short while ago, at the tree farm they'd had so much fun together. She'd enjoyed the time they'd spent among the evergreens and she'd thought things between them were finally on the right track.

But now they seemed to have backpedaled in a hot hurry. All because Rand had a problem with faith.

She accepted his offer and they exchanged brief, ultra-polite goodbyes. She locked the door and leaned back against it, the strain draining right from her body.

The funeral would be hard enough to deal with. Rand's grim presence at her side wasn't going to make it any easier. She had more reasons than she cared for to dread the morning.

Cate let Rand guide her by the elbow to the sanctuary. The hushed conversations in the large church only heightened the solemnity of the moment.

She shuddered as they slipped into a pew. "It's so sad."

A glance showed his rock-hard jaw.

This time, she didn't back down. "It's so different when it's a child. An older person has lived a full life and is ready to go home to the Lord. A teen hasn't even started to live. And to think a bad choice, a sin—"

Anger narrowed his eyes to blue slits. "It's a crime, Cate. She broke the law. If she'd upheld the law, she'd be alive, not heading to face your God who wasn't there for her, who didn't prevent her death. That same God who let Sam kill my cousin and your sister. And for what? What did their deaths accomplish for 'His Kingdom'?"

She winced at the heat in his voice and prayed for the right words. "It's true that God's all powerful and He can stop anything before it happens. But He wants us to love Him enough to do what's right because of that love, not out of duty or fear."

"Sure, I know there's choice, but I also have the choice to intervene—and do as often as possible. I'd rather work to catch the dealers before they get to the kids rather than preach about the love of a distant God who lets this—" he waved toward the altar "—happen."

"No one succeeds all the time. Even law enforcement doesn't. God could always yank strings to make us respond, but He doesn't want puppets, Rand, dancing to His will."

He scoffed. "And how do you make a kid 'get' that?"

"That's why I took Alec up on his offer. I'm older, I've survived some pretty awful mistakes getting here. I think that might reach the kids. Plus, I hope they can see how I live out the freedom I find in Christ, the freedom I didn't find by walking away from God."

"Again, how? How do you convince anyone that rules equal freedom?"

"I've been where these kids are. And I know God can use the mess I made to show how *not* to live life."

She gave him a pointed stare. "And I'm going to find whoever's stealing their futures."

"More power to you."

"God's power, not mine—"

The organ played its first chord. Cate looked around, certain the person who'd supplied Marly was among them. The dealer had to be close to the kids. By the same token, only someone close to the kids would uncover the dealer's identity. Was she the one who'd do it?

Cate felt certain she'd been attacked because she'd frightened the dealer. Without knowing his identity, even without knowing which, if any, kids she might keep out of his web, she knew she had to do something about all this.

She hoped to start by reaching Phil. Cate had done some research on the Web the night before and from what she'd learned, she suspected Marly had started using to compensate for her extreme shyness, when she became interested in Phil. Drugs offered a false sense of confidence.

Cate hoped she could impress the former soccer star with the urgency of the moment. They had to catch the dealer before another kid OD'd.

Twelve high school students carried the white casket to the simple wooden altar. Pastor Art Reams, his wire-frame glasses askew, eyes rimmed with dark circles, led the congregation in prayer. The choir sang much-loved hymns and the praise and worship team led in some of Marly's favorite songs.

And then, when Pastor Art began to speak of Marly, Cate welled up with her heartache. The broken promise of a life cut short hit her hard. Her tears flowed unchecked and she didn't try to stem her sobs.

To her surprise, a sturdy arm slid around her shoulders and a warm hand took hold of hers. She turned and through her tears, met Rand's blue, blue gaze. She leaned against him, absorbing his strength.

They might not agree on how they viewed God— and she would hold out hope it was only a matter of time before they did see eye to eye on faith again— but they did agree on the painful reality they faced. Someone was benefiting from tragedy and loss. Someone was making money. Blood money. Killing for the sake of greed.

They were going to stop him.

Together.

When the congregation began to thin, Cate marched up to Alec and pointed a finger at him. "You were wrong and I was right. We can't afford to trust one single program, no matter how good or comprehensive it might be."

Alec grabbed her finger. "We aren't just trusting one program. Parents are involved and the church gives the kids an outlet here. That's part of keeping them from bad influences."

"It's not working." She looked at J.J., who stood at Alec's side. "First, your three soccer players ruined their future with drugs." She turned to her fellow youth group leader again. "Now Marly has no future. She's dead, Alec. Dead."

He dropped his gaze. "I know. It's tragic, but I can't change that fact—"

"That's a cop-out and you know it." She cast a quick glance at Rand. His supportive nod gave her the courage to continue. "We have to *act*. Not just start a drug awareness and prevention program here for the kids, but also do something to wake up the parents. We have to give them the tools they need to fight this."

J.J.'s eyes were red from the service. "I'm with you," he said in a husky voice.

Alec raised both hands in surrender. "Adults aren't my field. You'll have to talk to Pastor Art."

"Great idea. I'll do that."

"I'm on board with Cate," Rand said. "And we can do a lot of good with the parents. But we need your help, Alec."

Cate caught her breath. Rand had just thrown down a challenge. Would Alec come through for the kids?

To be honest, Alec had disappointed her with his insistence on school-administered programs. The reality was, the church had to act. Even the man who'd turned his back on God had recognized the need to fight from more than one angle.

"Will you join us?" Rand asked. "I've come to work with the kids and I'll do whatever I can to give the parents the tools to help us fight. You can put your money where your guidance counselor mouth is and try to keep kids alive."

Alec's lips thinned. "Fine. I'll work with you. But I'm not sure overload is the way to go." With that, he walked away.

Cate, Rand and J.J. headed toward the door. "You guys can count on me," the coach said. "I'll do anything you need. It doesn't hurt to try."

Cate gave him a quick hug. "All that matters is that we not lose another kid."

When Cate and Rand reached the silver SUV, she turned to the silent man at her side. "So, Mr. Investigator. What's next?"

A smile tipped up the corner of his mouth. "You tell me, Tiger. You've been running this show all day long. I'm just glad I'm not Alec Hollinger."

She blushed. "You're the investigator—"

"*Arson* investigator, I'll remind you. Doesn't look like it was arson."

Cate thought for a second. "I'm ready to corner Phil, before he gets his defenses back in place."

Rand nodded. "You're right. I've suspected Phil knows more than he has said from the start. Phil it is."

She studied Rand for a silent moment, wondering if he were mocking her. Despite the levity of his response, she saw only sincere determination in his gaze. And something more. Something private and special—and theirs.

She smiled. "Phil it is."

In the church parking lot after the funeral, Cate and Rand waited for the congregants who'd returned from the cemetery to head toward the youth ministries building. A number of church families had set out a reception for Marly's family and friends.

As they waited, Rand's cell phone rang. He turned away to answer, but Cate could see how his features tightened as he listened to the caller. His side of the conversation consisted of nods, headshakes and a handful of monosyllabic responses.

When he turned back to her, a hint of red darkened his cheekbones and his jaw looked chiseled out of rough granite. "You'll be interested in this," he said, slipping his phone back in his pocket.

Cate drew a deep breath to brace herself, but Rand's expression told her nothing was likely to help. "Go on."

"The PD just got preliminary autopsy results on Marly. The coroner found trace amounts of rat poison. It doesn't look like any kind of accident."

Cate's world tilted off its axis. She felt sucker punched and if Rand hadn't reached out to bolster her, she probably would have fallen. When she could manage to spit out a question, she said, "Murder?"

"Looks like someone wanted our witness out of the way."

The implications were huge. "Then Sam…he was killed, too?"

"Possibly. Probably."

The car that followed her to Marly's house…the face at her kitchen window…the person who'd attacked her in the hospital. "Their killer is probably the same person who's after me."

Rand looked down at the ground for a moment, then lifted his gaze and met hers with those blue eyes. The intensity in their depths made Cate feel warm and protected.

"Maybe," he said. "But he's not going to get to you. We're going to get him first."

As Cate processed the latest information, she thought about Lindsay and the twins. Thank goodness she had someone like Zoe to look after them, someone she trusted completely.

She met Rand's gaze, where she saw understanding and a promise. "I think you're right." She glanced around the parking lot and saw groups of kids piling out of vehicles and heading toward the reception. "Let's go talk to Phil."

Moments later, the boy stiffened when Cate called out his name. His face revealed emotional ravages and when he realized she wanted to speak to him, he seemed much younger than his eighteen years of age. He said something to his companions, then jogged over to Rand and Cate.

"Hi, Miss Cate."

She placed a hand on his arm. "How're you doing?"

"I'm doing rotten."

"Sorry. I realize this is a tough time for you. But you do matter."

"It feels as though everyone thinks I'm the worst piece of scum in the universe."

He fell silent and Cate waited him out. Rand had the sense to keep his peace as well.

A minute later, Phil ran a hand through his mop of curly brown hair. "Yeah, well. Everyone figures because I was partying and Marly died from an overdose, that I stuffed her with drugs and killed her. Well, I didn't. I didn't give her anything. Okay?"

He stared at Cate and Rand, seeking agreement. His voice thrummed with intensity and Cate believed him.

Phil went on. "I quit using the night of the bonfire. I'm not stupid. I messed my life up bad enough. I didn't want to get stuck in jail on top of everything else." Pain radiated from his posture, his expression.

"And I didn't know Marly was using or trust me, I woulda said something to her."

Cate offered a silent prayer for wisdom and the right words. "That's got to be tough. And you say you didn't share your drugs with Marly?"

His jaw jutted. "It wasn't like *drugs,* Miss Cate. I just did Smurfs a couple of times, for fun. Not like doing drugs 'cause I'm a junkie or anything. And I never, *never* partied that way with Marly. Whatever she took, she took on her own."

Cate pounced on the opening he gave her. "So if you didn't give her whatever she took, then where would she have gotten it? Maybe the same place you got the…Smurfs?"

His expression changed as though a wall had dropped between them. "I don't know where she got…whatever."

Cate didn't miss what he hadn't said. "How about you? Where did you and your teammates buy the Smurfs?"

A flash of fear crossed his face. "I gotta go."

Phil turned and was about to follow the other kids to the youth ministries building when Rand caught hold of him. "That's not going to work, Phil. You ruined your chances for a spot on a college team and an athletic scholarship, but that's nothing compared to Marly losing her life."

The teen yanked his arm from Rand's clasp. "You think I don't know that?" he yelled. "I really liked her. She was my girlfriend." Tears filled his brown eyes. "Now she's *gone!*"

Rand crossed his arms. "She's gone and someone

sold her the junk that took her life. Help us find that someone before anyone else dies."

Phil blanched. "I can't help you."

"Can't?" Rand asked. "Or won't?"

With a shake of his head, Phil took off.

Cate groaned. "That didn't go so well."

Rand spun and shoved both hands through his hair. "It was a disaster."

"But…we know he didn't give Marly drugs. He would never have poisoned her either. I think he was telling the truth."

"I do, too, but we still have no clue where he got the Smurfs or where Marly got whatever she took."

"Did you think he was being loyal, or was he scared?"

"Scared."

"That's what I got, too." They headed toward the reception. "I think they're buying from an adult."

Rand opened the door for her and they walked into the gym side by side. "Someone with enough power to scare them. The question is who?"

She chuckled without humor. "That's the million dollar question."

TWELVE

In the gym, Rand and Cate went from group to group, expressing their condolences, listening to stories of Marly as a child, and as a gifted singer. Each time they came near, Phil shifted, heading for another group of kids who offered cover. His clumsy avoidance tactics, however, weren't going to get him off the hook.

"Are you hungry?" Rand asked Cate after a while.

"Not really. But I am thirsty."

"Let's go hit the punch table."

J.J. and Abby stood behind the cranberry-punch bowl, while Zoe and Alec manned the citrus and ginger ale drink.

"What a couple of weeks," Zoe said, draining a paper cup of her own. "How're you holding up, Cate?"

"Okay. I think." She scanned the room, caught sight of Phil staring at them, then took a sip from her drink. "Could be doing better."

"I'm going to miss her," Abby said. "In her own, quiet way Marly was a leader."

Cate turned to Zoe. "You'd better go relieve Miss Tabitha of my monsters. She's such a dear, but I don't want us to take advantage of her."

Zoe laughed and waved Cate's concern aside. "She and Mr. Graver were prepping for one of their cooking classes tonight. When I dropped them off, the twins had put on aprons and were all psyched to be the official taste testers. And Lindsay ran off to play with Miss Tabitha's cats the minute we got there."

Cate picked up another cup of punch. "Still, I can take the three munchkins off their hands for a while. I miss them. You'll be home so I can drop them off at your place later on."

"Of course. The kids and I are doing just fine, but for your sake, I wish this was all over and you guys could get back to normal."

"I hear you. At least, Dad is getting better. He's begun some rehab, even though his last skin graft was only days ago."

Zoe crossed her arms. "Until this creep is caught, nothing's going to be normal again."

"I beg to differ," Alec said. "One person's arrest isn't going to make a difference. So, normal? This is as normal as it gets."

Rand placed his fists on the white paper-covered table. "Are you suggesting we should do nothing?"

Alec took a step back. "No. No, of course, not. But one guy's arrest won't be the end of the situation."

The muscle in Rand's cheek twitched. "We do it one dealer at a time." He spun on his heel and started toward the doors. Then he cast a glance at Cate. "I'm heading out. You coming?"

She took her time to study the four behind the table, noticing Alec's reddened cheeks, Zoe's disbelief, Abby's frown, J.J.'s look of concern. She then put down her empty cup, and waved at the four behind the table. "I'm on my way."

But before she could take a step, wooziness hit her. She grabbed the table.

"Are you okay?" Rand rushed back to her side and slid an arm around her waist. "Let me get you a chair."

As always, Cate welcomed his warmth and support. She gave him a smile. "No, no. I'll be fine."

But as the minutes passed, her heartbeat sped up and a sense of restlessness overtook her. She waved away her friends' concern and tried to head toward the door, but with each step, she felt as though gravity had begun to fail her.

She stumbled into a lady with blue hair. "Oh, no! I'm so, so sorry. I didn't mean to hurt you."

"What is *wrong* with you?" Zoe said.

Abby placed cool fingers on Cate's forehead. "You feel a little warm. Are you coming down with something?"

Cate shook her head, but had to grab hold of it. Choppy sensations made her feel…weird. A wave of nausea hit her and she had the sensation of a growing distance from those around her, although she could see they weren't particularly far away.

As the seconds—hours?—passed, she felt a greater detachment from the world around her. Echo-like visual effects overtook her sight. People surrounded her, but she couldn't recognize them, no matter how hard she stared or tried to remember names. She heard voices, but they, too, struck her as incomprehensible. Odd items, a spoon, a tree, a pumpkin pie, danced before her, but when she reached out, her hand got there seconds after they'd waltzed right out of her grasp.

"Where…am…I…?" Confusion filled her.

As she floated in an indistinct, flimsy world, sleep overtook her, even though her chest hurt from the pounding of her heart. Everything went a lush, rich, velvety black, the sound of unearthly music—loud, crisp, clear and vibrant—ringing in her head.

Rand watched doctors and nurses work on Cate. They chased him out of the ER cubicle while they pumped her stomach, but he wouldn't let them keep him away once they'd finished their more invasive treatments. The good news: She would be fine once the effects of the drugs dissipated.

The bad news: Cate had overdosed.

His sense of betrayal overwhelmed him. How could he have let down his defenses to such a degree? How had he let himself care so much that this…this nightmare hurt so bad? He'd known her past. He'd known how easy it was for drug users to backslide.

How could he have fallen in love with a user?

Anger and disappointment joined his sense of betrayal. He didn't want to feel so much, but he did. For the woman fighting for her life.

How? How could Cate have been so deceitful? After all those nice speeches she'd made about poor choices and sin and repentance.

Still, no matter how hard he tried, he couldn't make himself not care, no matter how angry he was, no matter what she'd done. It mattered to him that she recover, that she get clean again. Not just for the sake of the investigation, but also for her sake. She needed to start over for real.

Even though he couldn't see their relationship going any further now. Not knowing the beast that ruled her life.

Her past had been hard enough to set aside for the sake of a future. He couldn't be sure exactly where they might have been headed, but he knew he'd felt more than just a passing attraction for Cate Caldwell. He hadn't admitted it even to himself, but thoughts of rings and weddings had begun to pop up.

Now?

He shuddered. So much for her so-called faith.

The kids…at least they'd been with Miss Tabitha when Cate collapsed. They hadn't had to witness their aunt's intoxicated condition.

Rand propped his elbows on his knees and buried his face in his hands. What a nightmare! As he sat there, listening to the beep of the monitors, a whirring caught his attention.

When he looked up, Joe had rolled his brand-new wheelchair into the room. "How is she, son?"

"She's going to be fine, physically."

Joe nodded. "Yep. Physical's one thing. I worry what this is going to do to her head. Poor kid. D'you know yet who did this to her?"

Rand gaped. "What are you talking about, Joe? Cate overdosed. She started using again."

Joe turned his gaze from his motionless daughter and fixed it on Rand. "Never in a million years. She might have joined in with the drinking back in high school, but Catey never did drugs. Someone deliberately drugged my daughter."

A spark of hope sprang up in Rand. He forced it back down.

Joe continued. "I haven't seen firsthand what she's been going through lately, but I do know her. And I know how she's changed over the years, how she lives her life and what really matters to her. I also know the God she serves."

"How can you even talk about God?" Rand said. "What has God done for you? He didn't prevent Mandy's death and he hasn't kept Cate clean."

"It's not about God stepping in and plucking Mandy from a blazing car, nor is it about God jumping into Cate's life. It's about faith. And I know Cate's living her life based on that faith."

"Faith…" Rand shook his head. "It doesn't mean a thing."

"It means everything. God made His children a bookful of promises and if you let yourself trust Him and those promises, then you'll reap the blessings He has for you. I don't have my daughter Mandy at my side these days, but before she died, I didn't have my daughter Cate. The way she was going, we were losing her."

"So you let God take one to keep the other. That seems like a lousy bargain."

"It's not a bargain, Rand. And that's not what I meant at all. It's the consequences of a series of actions. We'll never know until we're at His side the full impact of Mandy and Ross's deaths. Those deaths turned Cate around, but we don't know how many other kids might have thought twice about getting high. We also don't know how many lives Cate will impact with her ministry."

Rand found himself wanting to believe what Joe said about Cate. But…dare he? Dare he believe in the change father and daughter ascribed to a God Rand couldn't touch or see or hear?

"Trust me, Rand. She's not doing drugs and there's no way she's selling. She joined Alec Hollinger in leading the church's youth group to reach out and keep kids from heading down that path. That's her ministry."

"For your sake—" and Rand's, if he were totally honest "—I hope you're right."

Cate's weak voice pierced his argument. "I…don't…"

He ran to her side. "How are you?"

"I'd be better…if you didn't think…such stupid things…"

"You were tripping on dextromethorphan. And it was a bad trip. I'm not 'stupid' enough to think you chugged bottles of cold medicine by mistake."

Cate sighed, sounding exhausted. "I was fine until I drank that punch. Someone…someone spiked it."

"Really? You're trying to tell me three teachers and your best friend got together to drug you?"

Cate cranked up her bed. "No conspiracies, Rand…and Zoe's had nothing to do with it. One of the teachers…one of them's selling drugs to kids. Just think about it. Look at the access they have."

Rand narrowed his eyes. "That's quite an accusation."

"Think, Rand." Cate's voice grew stronger by the minute. "Teachers are in constant contact with teens, the biggest customer base for a dealer. J.J.'s soccer players…Alec's youth group…Abby's Future Homemakers…"

"*Your* youth group, *your* babysitter."

She held up a hand and ticked off fingers. "A student at the school as your primary witness…a melted school ID…three teachers with ties to the kids serving the punch I drank."

Rand tried to get his head around what she was saying.

Her smile struck him with its sadness. "My past history's just that, the past. I turned my life over to God and have never looked back." She tipped up her chin. "Tell me this. How carefully have you looked into their lives? Scour their pasts as thoroughly as you have mine. Who knows what you might find."

"Why would they have drugged you in a public place?"

"Why would the dealer attack me at the theater? Why would he follow me to Marly's house? Why would he grab me at the bonfire? Why would he try to gas me to death and smother me? I think it's pretty clear I've come close to whoever's dealing, maybe by befriending Marly. I've threatened them without even knowing it."

"So who're you accusing?"

"I don't know—yet."

"Then how can you suggest your punch was drugged?"

"Because it's the only thing I had since breakfast. Besides, you've been with me the whole time. Think about it. When did I have a chance to take any drug?"

"You hadn't eaten all day?"

She shook her head.

"No wonder that stuff hit you so hard."

"Test my cup, Rand. I'm sure it'll come back positive."

For a moment, Rand wavered. "Okay, how am I supposed to identify which cup was yours?"

She seemed to concentrate, try to remember. "You know what? I was still holding the cup in my hand when I started to feel bad. Maybe the EMTs know where it went."

"That's not much help—"

"It's all the help I can give you. You might just have to trust me. Find whoever spiked my drink, Rand. That's when you'll figure out who killed Marly and Sam."

"She's right," Joe said, breaking his silence. "Go track down the cup. They might still have it in the ER." The older man sighed. "I know you've had your sights on Cate from the start. You've wasted a lot of time, son, so get rid of that old, old chip on your shoulder. She's not the one."

Rand couldn't deny he wanted to prove Cate innocent. He also couldn't deny how much he wanted Joe and Cate to be right. But he refused to accept anything on faith. "I don't do blind faith. I'll let the evidence lead me to the truth."

"It seems to me, son, you don't do faith at all anymore. And that weakens you as an investigator. It may make you blind to the truth."

"How? How would a belief—faith—make me do a better job?"

Joe laid a hand on Rand's shoulder. "God's wisdom leaves ours in the dust. So does His strength. A man could do much worse than having the Lord as his partner on the job."

Rand stood. "I'll trust my training, if you don't mind."

Joe sighed again. "Just do your job. I'll do the praying."

"So will I, Dad," Cate added. "So will I."

Rand didn't answer. He opened the hospital room door and headed down the hall, his boss's words echoing in his head.

Could Cate be innocent after all?

In spite of what he feared, of the evidence—circumstantial, true, but evidence nonetheless—he hoped she was.

To Rand's relief, the EMTs had turned over all of Cate's belongings to the ER staff, including the paper cup she'd crushed in her hand. Rand bagged it and took it to Ethan, who arranged to have it tested right away.

"I believe Cate," the police chief said. "And something tells me that melted ID badge holds the key to the perp."

Once again, Rand played the devil's advocate. In truth, he no longer knew what he believed. He did, however, know what he wanted to believe. "But anyone could have left it at the theater at any point in time. It didn't have to be the night of the fire."

"True. But think about it. It was left by someone who hasn't reported a missing ID. What does that tell you?"

Rand had let that detail slide. He shouldn't have. Had he really been as biased as Joe and Cate felt? It looked like he could have been. "It might not tell us much…but then again, it might tell us the person hasn't needed the ID."

Ethan looked hard at Rand. "I'd be careful before I point a finger in Cate's direction."

"Too late," Rand said.

Ethan shook his head. "Then just make sure you get it right in the end."

Rand left the police station and went right to the high school. He agreed with Cate on at least one thing: Zoe Donovan had not drugged her drink. If Cate—and Ethan and Joe—were right, then one of the three teachers was their man. Or woman.

But after a frustrating three hours, Rand found himself right back where he'd started. Alec, J.J. and Abby were all concerned for Cate's welfare and none of them had hesitated to answer his questions. None had given answers that raised any flags.

He asked the sheriff for help researching the three teachers' backgrounds. The chief had already promised to call in a few favors, helpful because he'd worked with the DEA for so long.

Now Rand was stuck waiting for answers he hoped would help. Answers that could very well determine his future—with or without the woman he loved.

Cate convinced the doctor to release her well before he'd wanted to set her loose. She couldn't stand the thought of being stuck in the hospital one minute longer than necessary. Her throat still burned from whatever it was they'd used to pump her stomach and she still felt the effects of whatever she'd been given. But she could function and that would have to do.

She had a drug dealer to catch.

Before she started sleuthing, however, she'd decided to walk the short distance to Miss Tabitha's to see Lindsay and the twins. She hoped to catch them before they left for school. As she walked past the theater, she thought back on all that had happened since the night of the fire. Sam would never have the chance to straighten out his life, and Marly…it was too painful to think about.

A few blocks down from the theater, she walked past Rand's late father's bookstore. Brown paper still covered the wide windowpanes and she didn't think he'd done much work there since the fire.

Would he get back to it once he figured out the truth?

His suspicions hurt. And they shouldn't. She should never have let him matter so much.

But the reality was, she'd been falling in love with him almost from the start. She knew the attraction she felt wasn't one-sided—the kisses they'd shared had told her that. But a man who didn't trust her…one who rejected her Lord, rejected her. Unless Rand accepted the change God had made in her life, they could never grow any closer.

How could he even think to point the finger at her? He couldn't really think her capable of killing Sam and Marly? Could he?

Surely he wasn't that blinded by his work.

Or his lack of faith.

Cate took a deep breath and continued her walk. She'd never felt so lonely. She missed the kids. Of course, she'd spent time with them each day, visits that always felt too short, but leaving them with Zoe at night had been tough. She missed tucking them in, hearing their prayers—she even missed their early morning bickering. They would never think for even one minute that she'd take drugs, much less sell them to anyone else.

She prayed Rand would come to his senses, that he would somehow see the true her. And Lord willing, that he would see the truth of Christ shine through her. Maybe then he'd find a way to return to the faith he'd once had.

Ten minutes later, she reached Miss Tabitha's boarding house. Cate took the front steps with caution. She still felt a certain level of detachment, a sensation she assumed came from the drug she'd been given. It threw off her depth perception, and combined with her residual lightheadedness, left her less stable than she wished.

The sun had just begun to peek over the horizon as she rang the doorbell and she could smell winter in the air. She'd loved this time of year before the accident and in the years since, she'd prayed for God's peace to carry her through a season now filled with hard memories.

"Well, hello, there," Miss Tabitha said when she opened the door. "I heard you'd had another unfortunate incident, so I didn't expect to see you at all today."

"Couldn't stand to stay in that hospital bed another minute. I don't know how Dad's done it for so long. I—I just need to see the kids."

Miss Tabitha opened her arms to welcome Cate. The hug went a long way toward helping her feel better.

"Come on, honey," Miss Tabitha said. "Your three are in the kitchen, finishing their breakfast. Are you hungry?"

Cate sniffed and the scent of good food lured her deeper into the genteel home. "I'm not sure whether I can eat or not. They pumped my stomach, and even though I'm sort of hungry—maybe empty's the right word—I feel sort of queasy, too."

"Take your time. You can spend the day here with me.

You don't look so hot and I'd much rather be able to keep an eye on your color. Maybe your breathing, too."

Cate smiled. "You're just what I needed, Miss Tabitha. Let's see how I'm doing in a little while. Right now, I want to see the kids."

Miss Tabitha opened the swinging kitchen door. "Here they are."

"Aunt Catey!" Tommy yelled.

Robby stared. "Wow! You look rotten, Aunt Catey. You gonna puke or what?"

Both boys rushed to her, hugging her with all their strength. "Thanks for the welcome, guys."

"Have a biscuit, then," Robby said. "They're awesome."

Miss Tabitha winked. "How about I make you a cup of chamomile tea, Cate? That might make a much better landing than any kind of food."

"Sounds great." She looked around the bright, cheerful room. "Where's Lindsay, guys?"

"Oh, she went to feed the cats," Tommy said around a bite of ham. "She's always on the back porch with them."

"Go ahead, Cate," Miss Tabitha said. "Go see Lindsay. That girl's got a real gift with animals. I'll call you when your tea's ready."

Cate squeezed Tommy's shoulder and rumpled Robby's hair on her way to the back door. When she stepped outside, the crisp, spicy air soothed like a balm on her skin and for the first time in a long time, she felt something resembling normalcy.

Until she realized Lindsay was nowhere to be seen. "Lindsay? Where are you?"

No response.

She stuck her head back in the kitchen. "She's not here. You guys sure she didn't go back to the room?"

Tommy shrugged. "Didn't see her, but I'll call her—LINDSAY!"

No response.

Cate's phone rang. "Hello?"

"She's not there," a raspy, distorted voice said. "If you want her, you'll come meet me behind the church. Bring your fireman boyfriend and we'll make a trade. Lindsay for the two of you. And skip the cops. Or else."

THIRTEEN

"No, Rand!" Cate cried. "You can't drag in the police. No cops."

"You've been watching too much TV, Cate."

Anger surged, but she fought it back. It didn't matter what he thought or said. All that mattered was getting Lindsay back. "Are you going to help or are you going to seal my niece's fate with your lack of faith in me?"

She could almost see him wrestle with himself. "Okay. Wait for me. I'll be right there."

"I'm not going anywhere."

She hung up and sat back at the table. She didn't have the heart to make the boys go to school. At this time, Miss Tabitha's love and gentle comfort would do them more good than keeping up with their assignments. They had only one sister.

And Cate was going to get her back. No matter what.

She counted the seconds until Rand arrived. He greeted Miss Tabitha and the boys.

He asked everyone about Cate's phone call and Lindsay's disappearance and didn't even bother to hide his mistrust. But Cate was now past caring about that. She could only think about Lindsay.

Soon enough, she'd had her fill of his interrogations. "Lindsay's still out there. Are you ready yet?"

"I suppose."

"Let's get to the church, then."

They drove in silence. Cate prayed. She didn't want to focus on his shuttered expression, much less the thoughts that might be spinning through his closed mind.

His cell phone rang. "Hello?"

Cate tried to hear the garbled voice on the other end, but she couldn't.

"At the same time?" he said.

Silence. Then he nodded. "Did a great job fooling everyone, I'll grant you that."

Cate's curiosity surged, but she didn't dare make a sound.

He clapped the phone shut and slanted her a look. "We know who it is."

"Who?!"

"It's so hard to believe." He hit the gas and the SUV responded with increased speed. "Alec and Sam met in juvie jail years ago. Alec was in for theft—he'd been in and out of the system since very early on. He grew up in foster homes, from what Hal just said."

"Alec?" Cate shook her head in disbelief. "What's that about Sam? Sam didn't go through the juvenile system. He was tried as an adult."

"Only after the judge made that decision. Until then, he stayed in a youth facility. That's where he and Alec became friends. Now we know why Sam came straight to Loganton when he got out."

A hint of red colored Rand's cheeks and he reached for her hand. "I'm sorry, Cate. I owe you that much."

"Forget that for the moment. Lindsay's all that matters."

"Alec has her."

Cate's stomach dropped. "She's been through so much. Can we come up with a way to make the exchange without her seeing me go in?"

"Exchange? I do not intend to make any kind of trade with him. You're both coming out with me. The question is, will he come out, or will I have to drag him out?"

"That's even worse. Please don't make Lindsay witness a fight, much less a death. I don't think she could handle that."

"So will you let me call in Ethan and Hal? They're the ones who can keep that from happening."

Fear threatened. She refused to let it take root. She clung to faith. "Only if they come after she's free."

"They can't plan that—"

"Then let me take her place and you go bring in the cavalry when it's time."

"One thing's for sure. You're not going in alone." His voice had a tight edge and Cate suspected he was thinking of Mandy and Ross, and Marly, as well.

"What if that's the only way to free Lindsay and catch our creep?"

"Are you suicidal?"

"Not at all, but if it means Lindsay has a chance to grow up in a world with one less drug dealer, then I'm ready to see Jesus face to face. It's in His hands."

Rand drew a sharp breath. "Alec said he wanted both of us. We both go in. We can't take a chance. He'll hurt Lindsay if we don't do what he says. I'll punt once I'm there."

Cate met Rand's gaze, then slowly nodded. "Okay. We might have a stronger chance together. Two against one should give us better odds."

"Hopefully he's a lone operator."

"Don't forget, it won't just be you and me going for her. God's with me, and He counts for more than any number of creeps."

Rand averted his gaze. She went on. "Take my hand, please. Just be silent and let me pray."

For a moment, she thought he'd turn her down. Then, in an oddly hesitant way, he reached out and covered her fingers with his. "Do what you want."

"No, Rand. I'll seek and try to do His will."

To her relief, he didn't come back with a retort. Instead, he kept his gaze on her. *Father, please. Touch his heart with Your love.*

In a soft voice, she prayed. "Lord Jesus. We need Your wisdom and Your guidance here. Your protection, too. Lindsay needs Your comfort and a measure of Your courage wouldn't hurt her either. I confess I don't know what I'm doing, but You know what's best. Stop me before I blunder and push me through to where You need me to go. Bless Rand with peace and clear vision and let us know when we need that cavalry to come. In Your name, Amen."

To her surprise, a gruff "Amen" echoed hers. She squeezed his fingers before opening her door.

"Cate?"

She met his gaze. "Yes?"

"I wanted to believe you—"

Her phone rang, and she answered it quickly. "Yes?"

"What are you waiting for?" Alec said in his strange

muffled voice. "Come behind the new building. And your boyfriend better not have a gun on him."

He didn't have to voice his threat—Cate knew he'd hurt Lindsay if he felt he had to. "We have no weapons. Rand's a firefighter, not a cop."

"And you'd better not have called them either."

"I haven't."

"Come on, then. I don't have all day." He hung up. She turned to Rand. "We've got to go."

As they headed for the youth ministries building, Rand reached for her hand. "I'll get you both out. Trust me."

She smiled. "Funny thing is I do. I just wish you'd trust the One who loves you most."

He lowered his head. "I'm trying, Cate. I'm trying."

"Life is easier when you trust God."

Rand's silence hurt, but Cate couldn't dwell on it. They had a child to rescue.

In the shadow of the trees at the back of the church's property, they passed a car with an auto rental company's sticker on the license plate.

"He's planning to run," Rand whispered. "We have to be careful or he'll get away."

"I almost don't care, so long as he doesn't do it with Lindsay in the car."

He shot her a sharp look. "We want him in jail. We need him so we can go up the drug dealer food chain."

Cate squared her shoulders. She stepped ahead and without another look at Rand, called out. "I'm here. Let Lindsay go."

Cate's prayer hovered in the back of Rand's thoughts. So did her statements about decisions and consequences. On top of all that, he couldn't help but admire the courage she was now displaying.

Once upon a time, he'd believed. Then the accident happened. His faith had taken a dive after that. The years spent investigating fires in Charlotte hadn't shown him many examples of devoted believers. But he'd come home and he'd come face to face with Cate again.

He'd watched her for days—weeks—since the night of the fire. He'd seen nothing truly suspicious during that whole time, though he kept looking for it. Could he believe she'd changed into the mature woman he'd come to know, to admire, to love, through her relationship with God?

Or was he going to trust only what he could touch and see and hear?

Would today's Cate exist without faith?

He watched her step toward the cover of the trees, past the car parked in their shade. She carried her shoulders squared, her head held high and she took sure, firm steps. It struck him how well she knew herself, knew what she wanted, who she loved and yes, knew the God she served.

Rand envied her assurance right then. He knew she drew comfort and confidence from the faith she'd placed in God. The faith he'd shared once.

For the first time in many, many years, he felt a longing for that faith.

He took his first step. *Lord? If you're there, give me a hand.*

Cate stared at the man standing in the shadow of the new youth ministry building. "Why? Why would you do this, Alec?"

"Don't go there, Cate. I owe you nothing and you have no right to ask."

"I'm not buying that," Rand said.

Alec sneered. "And you think I owe *you* an explanation? I don't think so. You want Lindsay, then you'll both do as I say. Get in the car and I'll let her go."

"Let her go first," Rand said. "We're adults, she's a child. She has no defense."

The look on the guidance counselor's face spoke volumes. He had no intention of letting any of them go.

Cate stepped toward Alec. "Where is she?"

Alec shrugged. "She's okay."

"And I'm supposed to trust you? You've killed, taken advantage of the trust everyone put on you at school and at church and kidnapped my niece. Are you crazy? Where's Lindsay?"

Alec's mouth twisted in a grimace. "Get in the car. I'll let her go once you're there."

"I don't believe you." Cate didn't know where she'd come up with the daring—or insanity—to challenge him like that. "I don't believe you're going to do the right thing. Not after you've stooped to murder and dealing drugs."

He shrugged. "It's your gamble. Get in the car."

"And if I don't?"

He pulled out a gun.

Cate gasped. Her head swam. She felt sick again. Alec laughed.

She felt nauseous with fear. And the possible lingering effects of the drug she'd been given. "Oh…"

Then it occurred to her. What if…?

With another glance at Alec, she moaned again.

Then, as though unable to control her body, she sagged and swayed right where she stood. She had to help Rand. They had to get out of this mess. And this seemed the best option.

She relaxed and slumped against Alec.

He stumbled from the sudden shift in her weight, shoving against her with all his might. "Hey!"

She fell to the ground, hitting her forehead against something sharp and hard, her stomach clenching in an effort to brace her fall. She felt awful again.

But her ruse had given Rand the distraction he'd needed. He leaped at Alec.

As Cate's innards twisted and churned and her head swam, she heard the sounds of a fight, groans, grunts and the pounding of fists. A fleeting thought of helping Rand sped through her mind, but the reality of Lindsay's situation overtook any such consideration. Cate would have to trust Rand and God. She had to take care of Lindsay.

A whimper caught her attention. It came from the car. She dragged herself upright, arms wrapped around her middle. Then stumbled backward, avoiding Alec's wild grab in her direction.

"Where are you going?" Rand yelled then landed another blow to Alec's chest.

"Lindsay…" Every movement made her dizzier. A moan tore from her lips. A glance at the front and back seats revealed an empty car. A sticky substance rolled down the side of her face. Cate realized she was bleeding, but she couldn't do anything about it right then.

The whimper came again. Cate knew where Alec had stashed her niece.

She stumbled around to the rear of the car, stuck her hand under the latch and popped open the trunk. There, tied with blue-and-white nylon rope, lay Lindsay, a rag in her mouth.

Cate fought another wave of nausea. With every ounce of strength she had left, she reached in, and hauled out the little girl. "I got her!"

"I got him!" Rand answered.

Her legs wobbled and, child in her arms, she let gravity have its way. She fell on a bed of fallen leaves, praising her God.

Hal, Ethan and an army of officers of various kinds descended on the church. An ambulance roared up and Lindsay was loaded in. In spite of her objections, Cate was also strapped to a gurney and rolled in next to her niece.

Before the EMT slammed the door shut, Rand slipped in and sat at her side. He took her hand and pressed his cheek against her fingers.

"I'm sorry," he whispered. "I don't know if you'll ever be able to forgive me, but I was wrong. From the start."

Cate tried to chuckle, but found her stomach still too unstable. "Does that mean I get to hold this over you?"

"Aunt Catey!" Lindsay cried. "That's soooo wrong. You always tell me I gotta forgive the twins 'cause they don't know no better, since they're just boys. Mr. Rand doesn't know no better, you know. He's just a boy."

Cate gaped. She hadn't heard Lindsay say so much at one time since…well, ever. And then she realized what the little girl had said. She stole a glance at the "boy" at her side and caught his effort to stifle a laugh.

She smiled. "From the mouths of babes, don't you think?"

"Works for me." He waited.

"I think forgiveness is in my bag of tricks." She studied him, then squeezed his hand. "Just trust me, please."

"I'm there. Didn't do it the way I should have, but I'm there."

She studied him through narrowed eyes. "Anything else on the trusting front?"

He gave her a slow nod. "Yeah. I have some fence mending to do with God. But I did take my first step on the road back to faith today."

"I'm glad. I'm really glad."

"Can we have a do-over?"

"What do you mean?"

He cleared his throat. "Miss Caldwell. It's a pleasure to meet you. I've heard wonderful things about you and would love to get to know you much, much better. How about dinner once you're hale and hearty again?"

"You're going to make me wait that long?"

"Huh?"

Cate chuckled. "How about a barbecue on Friday night. The kids and I will do the honors. You come and we'll take it from there."

"I'll be there." He took a deep breath. "And I'll meet you Sunday morning at church."

"You have yourself a deal."

He sealed the deal with a kiss.

EPILOGUE

The Tuckerpalooza went off without a hitch. Cate spent the day checking on the teens in their many colorful booths. Only occasionally did anyone bring up the reason for the benefit, while a number of the youth-group members joined her in prayer for Marly's family and those who might still be caught in the grips of substance abuse.

Cate's father, by now an expert in his spiffy wheelchair, hadn't missed a beat. He had insisted on setting up and running his favorite booth. He'd armed himself with a dozen fishing rods and two dozen bowls, and then filled the bowls with cardboard slips. In this version of the traditional carnival game, instead of the typical cheap, plastic toy prize, players "won" the opportunity to volunteer to do any of a variety of jobs for the Tuckers.

Granny Annie, the town's diner owner, had donated buckets full of her trademark Sloppy Joes, which, as always, were selling well. Everyone in town had turned out to help, just as the teens had predicted. And while the elderly Tuckers, who had come to watch the festivities, weren't well enough to participate in much, Wilma in her wheelchair was everywhere.

At sundown, Rand appeared at Cate's side. "Tired?"

"Oh, yeah. But I'm so, so happy this worked out the way it did."

He grinned. "Let me tell you, I was sweating bullets."

"No reason. You're just running your first event, Mr. Youth Leader, you. How's it feel to be a star?"

"You're the star, Cate. You're the one who pulled it all together after Alec went to jail. You've even started a fund for Beth Hollinger and the triplets. I'm just in awe, and along for the ride."

She smiled, and leaned into the arm he wrapped around her waist. "Don't sell yourself short, Rand. You're doing a great job. Besides. What else could we do but take care of Beth and those little babies? Just because Alec had some screws loose in his past…I don't know. Scripture calls believers to care for widows and orphans. That's all I'm doing."

"Oh, I don't know about screws loose in his past. Crime is crime. It's pretty clear he had a neat little sideline business going, and he was afraid he couldn't trust Sam."

Cate shrugged. "I get that. But you have to have a screw loose somewhere to do what Alec did. If you don't trust someone, you don't just kill him. You break up the partnership and get yourself another partner."

"Ah…but that's where the crooked brain of a criminal eludes you, my love. Alec felt Sam was a loose end. He couldn't afford to trust him. He might turn against Alec, and—pow! The gig would have been up."

"Well, it's up now."

A couple of teens waved as they walked by, one of them carrying a soccer ball to the goal-kicking booth.

Cate waved back. "It's just too bad Alec and his pals provided a group of talented athletes the temptation that led to the ruin of potential careers. I'm surprised he broke down and confessed to everything, even to killing Sam."

"Hey, he's even turning on his higher-ups. We've gotten the names of some high-value dealers out of him."

Cate nodded slowly. "I hope you get them all. Just think of all the ruined lives—and I don't mean soccer careers. I mean, there are many, many Marlys out there."

"That's true, and that's the ultimate tragedy in drug crime. But we have to look at everything. Even while they're treading the waters of their loss, the boys have done the right thing. They've all come forward to testify against Alec. It took courage and internal strength to do that, even in the middle of the mess they've made for themselves."

Cate reached out and patted Rand's cheek. "We serve a mighty God. He can take evil, and in His own way and time, use it for good."

He sighed. "I'm beginning to realize I don't know anything about the extent of God's awesomeness."

"He loves to teach His children. I learn more each day I walk with Him."

"And I'm just following your lead. I suppose I'll learn more and more as I try to catch up." He pulled her close. "About following your lead… I want to join you for the long run. How about turning our crime-fighting, youth-group-leading partnership into something else? Something more permanent."

She drew in a sharp breath. "Rand? Are you…?"

"Yeah. I might not be the most romantic guy around,

but I've come to know the woman you really are. I'd be a fool if I let you go. Will you marry me, Cate?"

She reached up and cupped his lean cheek in her hand. "Yes. I'd love a long, old-fashioned engagement. I want to make sure we do this right. Let's pray and grow together and plan the wedding of my dreams."

"The marriage of my dreams."

* * * * *

Dear Reader,

Having grown up in a very cosmopolitan capital, Caracas, Venezuela, small towns have always held a certain appeal for me. I suppose that is why my husband and I have chosen to raise out sons in, well, small-town America. Today, however, small towns deal with the same problems as our major cities, and those are the kind of stories in my CAROLINA JUSTICE series; *Someone to Trust* is the last book of three.

I hope you've enjoyed getting to know Cate and Rand, both of whom grew up in a small town, left—Cate for a shorter time than Rand—and returned, each bearing wounds that need healing. My wish for you is that you'll turn to God for comfort in your walk through life. Love and joy are to be found in and through Him.

Blessings,

QUESTIONS FOR DISCUSSION

1. None of us are immune from making terrible choices, some worse than others. Cate made many as a teen, but she has since taken responsibility for her actions and repented. How do you generally react when you realize you've erred?

2. Rand judged a teenage Cate by the image she portrayed. Was it fair to her? Why or why not?

3. When Rand returns and sees the "new" Cate, he can't help remembering the teen she once was. Have you ever had a similar image problem? If so, how did you handle it?

4. Cate felt the need to prove herself, not just to her neighbors, but especially to Rand. How would you counsel someone in her position?

5. Rand felt distanced from God as a result of the accident that took his cousin's life, and the tragedies he witnessed as an arson investigator. How have you come to grips with the reality that God, while all-powerful, doesn't always respond to tragedy as we would wish He would?

6. Alec, like many other criminals, felt his misdeeds were justified by his past. How does your faith keep you from losing perspective when you bear painful wounds?

7. Some people, while they profess faith in Christ, feel certain commands don't apply to their particular situation for many reasons. If you find yourself in the company of such a person, how would you respond to their position?

8. If you were in a position similar to Rand's, would you feel as he does about Cate raising the three orphans? If so, why? If not, why not?

9. Have you ever been involved in a benefit like the Tuckerpalooza? If so, what led you to participate? If not, what's held you back?

10. Substance abuse by teens is an epidemic in our country, particularly with prescription drugs. Have you taken any steps to help those fighting it? If not, would you? What would hold you back?

11. Evidence shows that some people in particularly stressful careers, like firefighters and law enforcement personnel, build walls around their emotions to protect themselves from the difficult situations they confront daily. How would you respond to someone like that?

12. Raising children is tough. Raising someone else's is infinitely more so. How would you handle a situation like Cate's?

13. Joe Caldwell, Cate's father, mentored the teenage Rand. Scripture calls for mature women to mentor younger ones. Have you been mentored? Are you a mentor? If so, how has the relationship impacted your life? If not, would you consider doing so?

14. Cate trusted Alec, but he proved to be unworthy of that trust. Have you been betrayed by a friend? If so, how did you handle the relationship after you uncovered the betrayal?

15. If you live in a small town, what do you particularly appreciate about the place where you live? If you live in a large city, how do you view small-town life? Would you switch?

* * * * *

Dumped via certified letter days before her wedding, Haley Scott sees her dreams of happily ever after crushed. But could it turn out to be the best thing that's ever happened to her?

Turn the page for a sneak preview of
AN UNEXPECTED MATCH
by Dana Corbit,
Book 1 in the new
WEDDING BELLS BLESSINGS *trilogy,*
available beginning August 2009
from Love Inspired®

"Is there a Haley Scott here?"

Haley glanced through the storm door at the package carrier before opening the latch and letting in some of the frigid March wind.

"That's me, but not for long."

The blank stare the man gave her as he stood on the porch of her mother's new house only made Haley smile. In fifty-one hours and twenty-nine minutes, her name would be changing. Her life as well, but she couldn't allow herself to think about that now.

She wouldn't attribute her sudden shiver to anything but the cold, either. Not with a bridal fitting to endure, embossed napkins to pick up and a caterer to call. Too many details, too little time and certainly no time for her to entertain her silly cold feet.

"Then this is for you."

Practiced at this procedure after two days back in her Markston, Indiana, hometown, Haley reached out both arms to accept a bridal gift, but the carrier turned and deposited an overnight letter package in just one of her hands. Haley stared down at the Michigan return address of her fiancé, Tom Jeffries.

"Strange way to send a wedding present," she murmured.

The man grunted and shoved an electronic signature device at her, waiting until she scrawled her name.

As soon as she closed the door, Haley returned to the living room and yanked the tab on the paperboard. From it, she withdrew a single sheet of folded notebook paper.

Something inside her suggested that she should sit down to read it, so she lowered herself into a floral side chair. Hesitating, she glanced at the far wall where wedding gifts in pastel-colored paper were stacked, then she unfolded the note. Her stomach tightened as she read each handwritten word.

"Best? He signed it *best?"* Her voice cracked as the paper fluttered to the floor. She was sure she should be sobbing or collapsing in a heap, but she felt only numb as she stared down at the offending piece of paper.

The letter that had changed everything.

"Best what?" Trina Scott asked as she padded into the room with fuzzy striped socks on her feet. "Sweetie?"

Haley lifted her gaze to meet her mother's and could see concern etched between her carefully tweezed brows.

"What's the matter?" Trina shot a glance toward the foyer, her chin-length brown hair swinging past her ear as she did it. "Did I just hear someone at the door?"

Haley tilted her head to indicate the sheet of paper on the floor. "It's from Tom. He called off the wedding."

"What? Why?" Trina began, but then brushed her hand through the air twice as if to erase the question. "That's not the most important thing right now, is it?"

Haley stared at her mother. A little pity wouldn't

have been out of place here. Instead of offering any, Trina snapped up the letter and began to read. When she finished, she sat on the cream-colored sofa opposite Haley's chair.

"I don't approve of his methods." She shook the letter to emphasize her point. "And I always thought the boy didn't have enough good sense to come out of the rain, but I have to agree with him on this one. You two aren't right for each other."

Haley couldn't believe her ears. Okay, Tom wouldn't have been the partner Trina Scott would have chosen for her youngest daughter if Trina's grand matchmaking scheme hadn't gone belly-up. Still, Haley hadn't realized how strongly her mother disapproved of her choice.

"No sense being upset about my opinion now," Trina told her. "I kept praying that you'd make the right decision, but I guess Tom made it for you. Now we have to get busy. There are a lot of calls to make. I'll call Amy." Trina dug the cell phone from her purse and hit one of the speed dial numbers.

Haley winced. In any situation, it shouldn't have surprised her that her mother's first reaction was to phone her best friend, but Trina had more than knee-jerk reasons to make this call. Not only had Amy Warren been asked to join them downtown this afternoon for Haley's final bridal fitting, but she also was scheduled to make the wedding cake at her bakery, Amy's Elite Treats.

Haley asked herself again why she'd agreed to plan the wedding in her hometown. Now her humiliation would double as she shared it with family friends. One in particular.

"May I speak to Amy?" Trina began as someone answered the line. "Oh, Matthew, is that you?"

That's the one. Haley squeezed her eyes shut.

* * * * *

*Will her former crush be the one
to mend Haley's broken heart?
Find out in AN UNEXPECTED MATCH,
available in August 2009
only from Love Inspired®.*

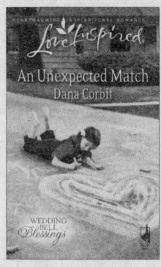

REQUEST YOUR FREE BOOKS!

2 FREE RIVETING INSPIRATIONAL NOVELS
PLUS 2 FREE MYSTERY GIFTS

YES! Please send me 2 FREE Love Inspired® Suspense novels and my 2 FREE mystery gifts (gifts are worth about $10). After receiving them, if I don't wish to receive any more books, I can return the shipping statement marked "cancel". If I don't cancel, I will receive 4 brand-new novels every month and be billed just $4.24 per book in the U.S. or $4.74 per book in Canada. That's a savings of over 20% off the cover price. It's quite a bargain! Shipping and handling is just 50¢ per book.* I understand that accepting the 2 free books and gifts places me under no obligation to buy anything. I can always return a shipment and cancel at any time. Even if I never buy another book, the two free books and gifts are mine to keep forever.

123 IDN EYM2   323 IDN EYNE

Name _____ (PLEASE PRINT) _____

Address _____ Apt. # _____

City _____ State/Prov. _____ Zip/Postal Code _____

Signature (if under 18, a parent or guardian must sign)

Mail to Steeple Hill Reader Service:
IN U.S.A.: P.O. Box 1867, Buffalo, NY 14240-1867
IN CANADA: P.O. Box 609, Fort Erie, Ontario L2A 5X3

Not valid to current subscribers of Love Inspired Suspense books.

Want to try two free books from another series?
Call 1-800-873-8635 or visit www.morefreebooks.com

* Terms and prices subject to change without notice. Prices do not include applicable taxes. Sales tax applicable in N.Y. Canadian residents will be charged applicable provincial taxes and GST. Offer not valid in Quebec. This offer is limited to one order per household. All orders subject to approval. Credit or debit balances in a customer's account(s) may be offset by any other outstanding balance owed by or to the customer. Please allow 4 to 6 weeks for delivery. Offer available while quantities last.

Your Privacy: Steeple Hill Books is committed to protecting your privacy. Our Privacy Policy is available online at www.SteepleHill.com or upon request from the Reader Service. From time to time we make our lists of customers available to reputable third parties who may have a product or service of interest to you. If you would prefer we not share your name and address, please check here. ☐

Love Inspired®
SUSPENSE

TITLES AVAILABLE NEXT MONTH
Available August 11, 2009

SPEED TRAP by Patricia Davids
The fatal crash was no accident. The only mistake was leaving behind a four-month-old survivor. For the boy's sake, Sheriff Mandy Scott *will* see justice served. Yet Mandy finds herself oddly drawn to her prime suspect—the boy's father, Garrett Bowen. If Mandy trusts Garrett, will he shield her from danger, or send her racing into another lethal trap?

FUGITIVE FAMILY by Pamela Tracy
Framed for murder, Alexander Cooke and his daughter fled to start a new life. A life that brings Alex, now Greg Bond, to charming schoolteacher Lisa Jacoby. Then the true killer returns. This time, Alex can't run. Because now he's found a love—a family—he'll face anything to protect.

MOVING TARGET by Stephanie Newton
A dead man on her coffee shop floor. An ex-boyfriend on the case. Sailor Conyers has murder and mayhem knocking at her door. She'll need her unwavering faith and the protection of a man from her past to keep her from becoming the killer's next target.

FINAL WARNING by Sandra Robbins
"Let's play a game..." Those words herald disaster as radio show host C. J. Tanner is dragged into a madman's game. Only by solving his riddles can she stop the murders. And only Mitch Harmon, her ex-fiancé, can help her put an end to the killer's plans.

LISCNMBPA0709